HOW TO BE

FREE

DAISY MAY JOHNSON is a writer, librarian and blogger. She writes about children's literature at *Did You Ever Stop To Think*, tweets as @chaletfan, and when she's not doing any of that, you'll find her curled up with her favourite school stories, or baking the world's best chocolate brownies. *How to Be Brave* and *How to Be True* are also available from Pushkin Children's Books.

HOW TO BE

FREE

DAISY MAY JOHNSON

PUSHKIN CHILDREN'S

Pushkin Press
Somerset House, Strand
London WC2R 1LA

The right of Louise Johnson to be identified as the author
of this Work has been asserted by her in accordance
with the Copyright, Designs & Patents Act 1988

First published by Pushkin Press in 2024

1 3 5 7 9 8 6 4 2

ISBN 13: 978-1-78269-440-3

Victoria sponge cake bullet point © Shutterstock / Ribkhan

Designed and typeset by Tetragon, London
Printed and bound in the United Kingdom by Clays Ltd, Elcograf S.p.A.

www.pushkinpress.com

"No girl is an island"   —JOHN DONNE

*(Technically he said: "No man is an island",
but he is not here right now to correct me.)*

THE VERY BEGINNING

This book is about three things.

1. Finding things. In particular, it is about finding a nun who goes missing and the three small girls called Hanna Kowalczyk, Calla North and Edie Berger who set out to find her and bring her home.

2. Family. A lot of people think that family is just the people that you are related to but it is so much more than that. Families can be made of the people you love, your pets, your friends, your favourite recipe for salted caramel truffles, and people that you've not even met yet.

3. Footnotes. This is not just because I enjoy things that start with the letter F but rather because I am very forgetful and footnotes allow me to add things in when I remember them. These things might be Additional Important Information, or Jokes, or Useful Things That You Should Be Aware Of. All you need to do is look for the

little number in a sentence (like this one[1]), and find the number at the bottom of the page that corresponds with it.

But before all of that, it is about a girl called Sarah Bishop.

[1] This is a footnote. You will see that it is the only footnote on this page and now, all you need to do is go back up and read the rest of the sentence on the page itself. I am aware that is a lot of information to take in so you are welcome to stop for a moment and have a biscuit before you do. I recommend a pink wafer.

A GIRL CALLED SARAH

There are several things that you need to know about Sarah Bishop and the first one is this: she was born in the last days of the First World War and so, for a long time, knew a world with no cake or sweets at all. This was because of a thing called rationing. Rationing was when the government gave people a booklet full of small coupons. These coupons could then be used to purchase things and make sure that everybody got everything they needed during the war. The only problem was that when those tickets were used up, people wouldn't have any left until the next ones were given out.

It took two years after the war for rationing to end. Sarah was two when it did and she watched as all of her neighbours and the people in her town embraced the freedom of a life without coupons and restrictions. Her parents, however, did not. They had been so saddened and broken by the events of the war that they did not quite know what to do with themselves. They would spend days trying to figure out what to say to each other and their daughter and failing entirely at both. And so they lived a quiet and small and sad life where they slowly withdrew from the world and all of the wonders that it had to offer. They ate plain and simple food, and refused social invitations and, when their sadness grew almost too much for them to bear, they would not even leave the house for weeks.

But then, one day, Sarah Bishop realized that there was another way to live.

This was all due to the work of Angela Anderson, her next-door neighbour. Angela's daughter was getting married and Angela had decided to bake a cake to celebrate the occasion. Angela was not a good baker and occasionally she was even catastrophic, but fortune had favoured her on this day and she had somehow managed to bake the sort of cake that you might find if you ever looked up the definition of "cake" in the dictionary. It was perfect. It was so perfect, in fact, that Angela had asked all of her neighbours to come around and witness it. She had rung the doorbell of old Miss O'Hara from Number 47, knocked on the door of Mr and Mrs Jacobson from Number 49, and even though she could not quite believe that she was doing it, she had invited around the strange and never seen out in public Mr and Mrs Bishop at Number 51.

Mrs Bishop had refused, of course. It was almost instinctive to her now. "I have to look after my daughter," she said. "And cook the supper. Then there's the cleaning. You know."

"It's eleven o'clock," said Angela Anderson, with a force that surprised her. "There's time for all of that yet. Come and look at my cake and have a cup of tea, and bring your daughter too."

She had seen the daughter going back and forth to school. Always by herself. Always far too pale for comfort. Never with one of her parents at her side.

"I don't know," said Mrs Bishop.

"Come," said Angela Anderson. "Please."

And for some reason that she did not understand, Mrs Eileen Bishop did. She brought her husband, George, dressed in his suit and as formal as a man going to church, and her small and wide-eyed daughter, Sarah, and when they had all finished staring at the wonder of Angela's perfect cake, the wide-eyed Sarah walked forward and calmly helped herself to a bite.

Sarah was punished, of course, but she did not care. And even when she *did* care about being confined to her room or fed meals even plainer and sadder than before, all that she had to do was remind herself of how that cake had tasted. She had never thought that something like it could exist in the world. She wanted to know everything about it. She wanted to understand it, completely, and she wanted to make her own.

And so, Sarah began to educate herself. She would visit the local library on her way home from school and when the librarian was looking the other way,[1] Sarah would sneak out of the children's section and into the adult room where the recipe books lived. They mentioned

[1] Librarians back then were very fond of rules and could often be a bit scary when they found people breaking them. Now, of course, they are some of the best people on the planet and you should always bring them cake to celebrate this.

ingredients that she had never tasted and places she had never heard of and sometimes, late at night, she would dream about the time that she might be able to make them for the people that she loved. She was not quite sure who these people might be and where she might find them but she knew with a definitive and sharp sense of sadness that they would not be her parents.

It was during one of her library visits that Sarah met Mrs Weisenreider, an elderly refugee from Germany, who had come over to England after the war and now spent her days reading cookery books to remind herself of all that she had left behind. Mrs Weisenreider was the one who taught Sarah about Springerle cookies, which were tiny little patterned biscuits that had been made in her Swabian village in Germany ever since the fourteenth century, and one day she gave Sarah the mould to make her own.

It was also Mrs Weisenreider who introduced Sarah to the other widows. They had come from all over Europe, "for love," said Mrs Van Dam, "for freedom," said Mrs Gladstone, "and not for the food," added Mrs Bertolini, as quick and as smooth as anything you'd see on the London stage. This always made the rest of them laugh and then Mrs Weisenreider would bustle the group out of the library and down towards the nearest café for a cup of tea and deeply inappropriate gossip. Sarah was always sent home for this part and so, the moment she was old enough, she got a job in the café so that she could gossip with them.

When Sarah was twenty-one, she was given the unexpected present of two new baby sisters named Georgia and Lily. One week after this, the Second World War began and with it came the death of her father. He had signed up with the navy in the first few weeks of fighting, unable to deal with the thought of this happening all over again and unable to let it happen without him being involved, and he had lost his life almost as quickly. And so when her friends were moving on to do war work and dig for victory, Sarah stayed with her mother to help her look after the twins and keep money, somehow, coming into their sad and broken house. She doubled her shifts at the café and when the air raids began, she started to work nights as well as an emergency telephonist.[1]

Somewhere, in the middle of all of this hustle and bustle, Sarah's mother died.

And that meant that Sarah had to become both mother and father to the twins even though she was barely an adult herself.

The widows helped her, of course, for they knew about what had happened and they all loved Sarah very much at this point. Mrs Weisenreider took in their washing to do alongside her own and Mrs Van Dam made enormous amounts of nourishing soup for them all to eat together while Mrs Bertolini and Mrs Gladstone sat down and

[1] This is a fancy word for somebody who answered the phone calls at the fire station after a raid and sent the fire fighters to where they were needed the most.

looked through all of the paperwork and bills that Sarah's mother had been ignoring for so, so long. It was then that they realized that things were about to go very wrong for Sarah and so they began to plot.

Their plot involved the sending of many letters to all of their friends and relatives scattered across Europe, and long conversations with each other at the café, and for a few months, Sarah did not know anything about it. She spent her days with the twins, and the love and help of the widows kept the three of them safe. She would talk about what the future might hold and dream of a bakery that might be her very own. "But I have to forget that now," she would say to whichever widow was sitting by her side, "I have the girls to look after and I'm the only person they've got."

One day, when Lily and Georgia were busy playing hopscotch with each other on the street outside, and the widows had received the final pieces of information that they needed, they took Sarah to one side and began the process of telling her everything.

"Sarah, my dear, we have something to tell you," said Mrs Weisenreider. "We all care for you so much and we love you as if you were our own family. And we know that your parents have not left you with enough money to live on. There are so many bills here and none of them have been paid for quite some time. Did your mother ever speak to you about money? Properly?"

"I thought we were managing with my extra shifts," said Sarah. "I didn't know things were bad."

"They are not good," said Mrs Weisenreider. "There are many bills that have not been paid and your father, before he died, took out a loan with the bank. That has not been paid back either."

Mrs Van Dam nodded. "There is no way that your shifts will cover all of what is owed. We have spent weeks trying to make the numbers work, but they will not. There is just not enough money."

"So we have been putting a plan together for you these past few weeks," said Mrs Gladstone at her gentlest. "And if you would be happy to accept our help, then we will give it to you."

"But you've already given me so much," said Sarah. "How can I ask any more of you than that?"

"But so much is not enough," replied Mrs Weisenreider. "Permit me to explain our idea to you."

And so she did.

I'LL NEVER FORGET YOU

The plan was this: train tickets to Cornwall for Sarah, Lily and Georgia; the promise of an apprenticeship in a bakery run by Mrs Bertolini's best friend's great-niece by marriage; and enough money to get Sarah started in a brand-new life doing the things that she had always dreamt of. It was the greatest gift that the widows could have given her and when Sarah protested it, when she told them that it was too much, they told her that they loved her and that she had to go.

"You have a life beyond this house and it is waiting for you to live it," said Mrs Van Dam in her quiet and gentle way, "and it is our joy to make it happen for you."

When Sarah protested again, Mrs Van Dam patted her knee, and Mrs Gladstone took her hand and Mrs Bertolini took the other while Mrs Weisenreider told her to write.

"Not every day," she said, "because you will not have time and we do not expect it of you. But when you can, please tell us how you are. Please remember us."

"I'll never forget you," said Sarah, and she didn't. She sent the first postcard from the bakery, the day after she had made panettone for the first time, her hands still aching from kneading the dough and her mind still full of its magic. She sent the others on a regular basis from that point on and the widows devoured each and every one of them. They learnt about how Georgia grew up into somebody who was clever and quick and about how she always asked Sarah questions that she never knew the answer to. They learnt about Lily and about how she was funny and stubborn and was always the first to be awake and the last to fall asleep. And they learnt about how Sarah was becoming the baker that she had always dreamt about being.

In turn, the widows sent Sarah postcards of their own. They told her all about the things that were happening in the local area and even though these were not often the most exciting or dramatic pieces of news, for Sarah they were perfect. She learnt about how the library had got new books, about a group of nuns who were setting up a convent just outside of the village, and about how to make the perfect sponge pudding even though rationing was back in effect and half of the ingredients were missing.

For a while, there was nothing but postcards flying back and forth and Georgia and Lily grew accustomed to trotting down to the post office with another one in their hands and returning with a fresh one for Sarah to read. Even Mrs Bertolini's best friend's great-niece by marriage had become interested and was starting to learn English as a result of them.[1] And when the postcards started to bring bad news with them, when one of the widows died

1 Her vocabulary was very good but rather cake specific.

17

and then the other, she was the first to wrap her arms around Sarah and help her through it all.

The last widow was Mrs Weisenreider, and even though her handwriting grew increasingly wild and her spelling even wilder, she wrote postcards right up to the end. For a while, both Sarah and Mrs Bertolini's best friend's great-niece by marriage[1] worried about why they might have stopped coming and then a letter arrived which explained it all. Mrs Weisenreider had died and left Sarah everything that she had.

And everything, along with all of the money that she had saved over the years, was just enough for Sarah to buy a small bakery of her very own.

"Where will you buy it?" asked Georgia.

And for the first time in her life, Sarah did not have to think about how to answer one of her sister's questions.

"Home," she said.

[1] Whose name was Giulia Ricci in real life but nobody used that, not even Giulia herself.

A CLOUD IN YOUR HANDS

Sarah and the twins, who were teenagers now and passionately devoted to the wellbeing of each other and their sister, left Cornwall in sunlight and returned to Little Hampden in rain. They bought a small bakery just down from where Sarah had met the widows for the first time and even though the library was now a shop and the café was now somebody's house, Sarah felt her heart warm whenever she walked past them. It was because of this that she named the bakery Bishop & Family[1] and every moment that she could, she told the twins about the widows and about how they had saved the three of them when everything had seemed so lost.[2]

The bakery opened on the first Monday of July. It was a good day to choose for this turned out to be the day after rationing officially ended again across the country and people could finally put their ration books aside and could go to the shops and buy what they wanted and without having to save their coupons up for weeks to

1 Just in case you do not know what an "&" is, it is a fancy way of saying "and" but putting a squiggle instead.

2 This bakery is going to be very important in everything that follows from this point so Do Not Forget It.

afford it. The people of Little Hampden celebrated with a party that saw them dance from one side of the village to the other, pausing only to buy everything that Sarah had baked that morning, before they came back the day after and then every day after that to do it all over again.

By the end of that first, giddy week, Bishop & Family was a success and Sarah knew that she and her sisters were at home. They turned one of the small attic rooms into a bedroom, patching curtains together out of old clothes and dust cloths, and painting the walls in all of the colours that they liked, before painting patterns on all of the tiles in the bathroom next to it and putting fresh flowers in a mug on the windowsill. Downstairs, they polished all of the floorboards until they shone and Lily taught herself how to make lace mats which she then placed underneath every cake in the window.

One day a woman from the council came into the shop. She explained that she was worried about how Georgia and Lily had not yet joined a school and needed to check if they were receiving a proper education. Sarah had pointed out that they were fifteen years old and even if they did join a school, they would be leaving it by the end of the year.[1] She then decided to also point out that the twins were fluent in Italian and English and a handful of other languages thanks to all of the tourists that had come into

[1] At this point in time, children could leave school when they were fifteen years old. Before this, children could leave when they were fourteen years old and many years before that, they could leave when they were twelve or thirteen.

Mrs Bertolini's best friend's great-niece by marriage's bakery, that they could do the sort of mathematics that you or I would need a piece of paper and several hours to work out, and that they could make pastries so rich and delicious that you would almost weep to see them. And if all this was not good enough, the two of them also volunteered in the bakery at the weekend and could serve a queue that went out of the door without breaking a sweat. The woman from the council was convinced by this argument and even more so when Sarah sent her home with a scone that was so gentle and soft that it was like holding a cloud in her hands.

Now, I know that you may be thinking at this point that "all of this is very lovely to read about but we were promised a missing nun and three small girls who are very good at finding things that are lost and you haven't given me anything that looks like that yet".[1]

But there are things you need to find out before we can get to that part.

Trust me, though. There was so much yet to come for Sarah and Lily and Georgia and June—

Ah. You don't know who June is yet.

Well, I'll tell you all about her now.

---

[1] Also you might be thinking, "This bakery sounds great but I am Quite Hungry now and you didn't prepare me for that in the slightest," and if you are, I really very much understand and recommend that you eat a pink wafer before the next chapter because it's only going to get worse.

KALE SOUP

One day the bakery door opened and a young girl ran inside.[1]

"Hello," said Sarah.

"Hello," said the girl. "I need your help. I'm running away from school."

"Which school?" Sarah asked calmly. "There's no school here in the village."

"It's up in the woods," said the girl. "Quite the hike really. Anyway, it's awful wherever it is. They make us eat kale soup. Can you imagine?"

Sarah pulled a face. "I'd rather not."

"I knew you'd understand," said the girl. She sighed in a rather resigned fashion. "Honestly, between you and me, I'm not very good at running away. This is my nineteenth attempt and I haven't got it right yet."[2]

---

1 And over sixty years later, that same girl would— Hang on. I'll tell you all about *that* bit shortly.

2 The selected highlights of June's previous Rather Poor Attempts At Running Away: buying tickets from and then being promptly sent back to school by Margaret-who-sold-the-tickets-at-the-train-station; being caught by the headteacher who was buying a sausage roll for his lunch and had Quite The Quick Reflexes when seeing an Unexpected Pupil walking by; and finally, missing the one bus out of the village because she was distracted by the smell of bacon sandwiches at the local café.

"So you came into a bakery," said Sarah. "Between you and me, I don't think this one is going to work out well either. Sorry."

The girl nodded. "It's because I want something nice to remember before I go back. I just walked right past one of my teachers and he looked at me and then I looked at him and all I could do was run and I've run a lot today because I had to get through the wood before anybody had noticed that I'd gone and now I've ruined everything. He's only minutes behind me. All I've got left are these last few minutes of freedom."

Sarah took a deep breath. "That's a lot to take in."

"I know," said the girl. "I haven't even *seen* cakes for weeks." She looked around her and visibly relaxed. Sarah had been baking bread that morning and the shelves were packed with her efforts. She had made Vienna bread and long, slender baguettes, tiny, twisty knot rolls and dusty white bread buns, and it was one of the most beautiful things that the girl had seen for a long while. "Do you bake everything here? I want to be a baker when I grow up. I'd love to have a bakery like this. Can you imagine? Nothing but Victoria sponge every day? Oh it would be perfect. Sorry. I'm babbling. It's just—it's so perfect in here. You must be so happy. Sorry."

"It's all right," said Sarah. "I understand how you feel. You don't have to apologize to me about that."

The girl gave her a quick, shy look. "Oh I *always* have to apologize."

"Not here," said Sarah. She had spent years trying to

figure out why the widows had saved her and now, all of a sudden, she understood. "What's your name?"

"June Mortimer," said the girl.

"My name's Sarah Bishop. You can come here any time you like."

"They'll never let me come back."

"They will," said Sarah.

The door to the bakery opened again. This time, it was for a tall and slender and deeply unimpressed looking man. He was very red in the face and had clearly run for much longer than he was comfortable with. He looked at June first and then at Sarah. "My apologies," he said, clearly meaning none of it, "but this girl is not supposed to be here. I will punish this runaway severely, you have my promise." And this part, he clearly meant.

"Hang on," said Sarah.

The man coughed. "I'm sorry, Miss—er—I don't know your name—?"

"Sarah Bishop, Mr—?"

"Mr Miniver," said Mr Miniver.

Sarah gave him a bright smile. "Mr Miniver, June wasn't running away in the slightest. She was coming here to get the food order to take it back to the school, just as she'd been asked to do.[1] And in fact, I know that June will be coming here every week to pick it up as well,

1 You will note that Sarah did not tell Mr Miniver who had given June permission to do this and that was because she was rather brilliant indeed.

but she was just telling me that she needed permission from one of the most senior and responsible members of staff such as yourself in order to do so."

Mr Miniver stared at her. "What?"

"It's all been arranged," said Sarah, who was rather enjoying herself. "So if you'll give June permission to come along every weekend to pick up the order for you all, I think I can find something for you to enjoy as well. A little extra. In fact, I insist. You look like the sort of man who deserves a pastry. A bonus. Something to eat outside while I get the order ready for June. Does that sound like a plan?"

Mr Miniver looked at her. He looked at June. And then he looked back at Sarah. "You wouldn't—you don't—happen to have any chocolate éclairs, do you?"

A CAKE HEART

When Mr Miniver went outside to eat his chocolate éclair, June did not breathe until the door had closed behind him. It was only then that she turned around and said to Sarah, "Why are you helping me?" It was such an unusual thing for adults to do, especially to people like her, that she was quite baffled by it.

"You remind me of my sisters. If they were ever in trouble like this, I'd want somebody to help them."

June looked suddenly interested. "Do they go to my school?"

"No," said Sarah. "They don't go to any school. I taught them everything I know and then we just get books for everything else."

A dreamy expression of longing passed over June's face. "I'd love that. Learning what you want to know. Do you know what my school is like? We learn about how to have neat handwriting and every now and then, if somebody wants to be really exciting, they teach us how to iron shirts."

"Your parents must have thought it was the right school for you, though?"

"Any school would have been the perfect school for me," said June darkly. "They'd have sent me anywhere that meant that I didn't go home for holidays. I haven't been home for years."

And it was then that Sarah said something rather unexpected. "How old are you?"

"Fifteen," said June, startled. "I only have a few months left at school until I can leave and when I do, I won't look back."

"Well then," said Sarah, who had been having an idea for the past few minutes and felt that now was the time to share it, "how about I offer you a job?"

And this was such a remarkable thing for her to say that June did not say anything at all.

Sarah continued. "When you leave school, you can have a job here. No questions asked. It's yours if you want it. Full time. Paid as well as I can make it. Until then, you can come every weekend and I'll teach you everything I know. You said you wanted to be a baker so I'm going to give you that chance."

June stared at her.

Even the thought of it was enough to fill her heart with hope.

"I'll make it work," said Sarah. "Every Saturday and the moment that you leave school, you can come here. I mean, only if you want—?"

"More than anything," said June. She could not quite understand how her world had been so painful and so wrong for so long and now, all of a sudden, it was finally starting to feel like it made sense. "I just don't understand why you're being like this to me."

"You'll understand it all one day," said Sarah. "But for now, start with this."

And she gave June a biscuit.

LIKE A PLAN COMING TOGETHER

And so June Mortimer began to visit the bakery every Saturday and even though it was just for a few hours, and sometimes for even less, those were the happiest days of her life. Sarah taught her how to make cakes speckled with chocolate chips, and how important it was to eat them when they were still warm from the oven rather than let them stand and go cold. She taught her about how sweet and fudgy dates could be, and how to make a sticky and rich parkin that tasted of bonfire night and fireworks, and how to make twists of pastry so crisp with sugar, that biting into them reminded you of the first frost of winter.

When June was not baking or waiting for her lift back to school, she would squeeze onto the back step of the shop with Lily and Georgia and the three of them would plan their future together because they knew that they would never be apart. The precise details of this future remained imprecise for some time until the great day when Georgia suddenly worked it out. She said, "We'll run a book-café," and it was all so startlingly perfect that Lily and June stopped everything that they were doing and paid complete attention. "We'll serve books and cakes and we'll stop everything for afternoon tea."

"Oh, yes," said June. She felt rather dazzled. "Yes. Of course. We couldn't do anything else. It's a wonderful idea. I'll bake and you can sell the books and Lily can look after people, and then Sarah can retire and take some time off and put her feet up."

"Well, we wouldn't let her do a *thing* at the café," said Lily. "She's so tired all the time, and she needs to rest. If she wanted to, she could lead a baking demonstration every now and then but that would be absolutely *it*."

Georgia nodded with approval. "Oh just imagine it—we would have cake *everywhere*."

"And everything that we sell would be wrapped up like a birthday present," replied June. She felt suddenly feverish with excitement. She could almost see it all right there in front of them. It was so real. "We could tie ribbon around every book when it's sold, and wrap it in tissue paper the same colour as well. And have little boxes for people to take away their cakes in. And we'd make miniature Victoria sponges too, just the perfect size for one person to eat *entirely* to themselves."

"And there'd be absolutely no kale," said Georgia, who had heard a lot about the catering choices at June's school.

"Or anything green *anywhere*," said Lily with a bright grin. "Unless it's icing."

"We should call it Bishop & Mortimer," said June.

For a moment nobody moved. In the distance, they heard the shop bell ring and then the sound of Mr Miniver chatting to Sarah. He had started turning up early to pick up June so Sarah had started to distract him with a chocolate éclair that had to be eaten before he left. It only gave June a few minutes extra with her friends but that day it felt like everything.

Lily reached out to take one of her hands and Georgia the other.

"To Bishop & Mortimer," said Lily.

"The three of us together forever," said Georgia.

"Forever," said June. "Forever."

THE BEGINNING OF A
BEAUTIFUL FRIENDSHIP

From that point on, the friendship between Georgia, Lily and June became as solid as stone. Georgia helped June out with her homework and the two of them would sit on the floor behind the shop counter as Lily helped Sarah make croissants for the Sunday morning rush. When the homework was done, Sarah would teach June about how to make the perfect ganache or how to make butter icing that was so tasty that June wanted to eat nothing else for the rest of her life. And at the end of the day, when they closed the shop at five p.m, they would sit together and eat anything that hadn't been sold before Mr Miniver arrived to take June back to school.

June held on to that friendship like gold and the memory of it got her through the long and lonely days at school. She would think of Lily and Georgia whenever they were served kale soup for lunch, and she would think of Sarah's warm and welcoming hugs whenever all of the other girls got a letter from home and she did not. And whenever all of this was not strong enough to keep her sadness at bay, she would pull out her notebook and fill it up with ideas for Bishop & Mortimer. She would sketch how the building and the menu might look and share this with Georgia and Lily at the weekend, and when they gave feedback or new ideas, she would spend the next week refining them.

June took the notebook down with her one Saturday to share her ideas for the perfect Victoria sponge. It was a particularly busy day and Sarah had been feeling tired so she did not get a chance to do this until late in the afternoon, only a handful of minutes before she was due to be picked up and taken back to school.

"I call this meeting of Bishop & Mortimer to order," said June. "We don't have much time so let's get straight to it. We need to talk about Victoria sponge." She gestured at one of the drawings she had made; a small and quite beautifully formed cake, dotted with strawberries and covered with a fine dusting of icing sugar. She had been working on it all week. It was one of the best things she'd ever drawn. The thought of baking it made her mouth water.

"We *always* need to talk about Victoria sponge," said Lily. "I think that can be one of our rules. If we can make them look half as good as you draw them then they are going to be a bestseller."

Georgia handed around biscuits and assumed a practical air.[1] "We're also going to need to think about the property

---

[1] You can tell when somebody is about to assume a practical air because they will start looking at something nobody else can see and saying things like, "Golly, Have You Ever Seen Such An Interesting Fuse Box?"

and maybe get in touch with some estate agents. It's never too soon to be aware of what's available. The only thing is that it can't be here. In the village, I mean. It has to be by the sea somewhere."

"Why can't it?" said June, suddenly baffled.

"Because everything tastes better by the seaside," said Lily. "When we were little, sometimes Sarah would take us to St Ives to swim. We'd walk just straight into the sea like—like you walked into the bakery today—not even changing our clothes or anything—and it was always so warm and the water was so clear and bright that it was like swimming in the *sky*."

Georgia let out a contented sigh at the memory. "Do you remember the time we went to the beach and then the tide came in and we had to get rescued by Sarah?"

"She bought us both doughnuts after though. It wasn't all bad."

"And definitely not as bad as kale soup," said June, who knew that Lily and Georgia could talk for hours like this unless they were distracted. They were just like Sarah. Listening to the three of them talk was like standing in a flock of birds, all of their words flying around you and leaving you breathless with excitement.

"There's loads of places we could look at round here," said Lily. "Filey. Cayton. Whitby. All the little villages in between. You don't even need your own car to get to them. You can get the train or the bus or even a boat. There's this place called Merlin Cove on the coast there that I read about once. You can only get to it when the tide is right and the wind is blowing from a certain direction and I'm not even sure that it's real but I want to find out—"

June looked confused. "Wait—if people can't find us, how will we ever sell anything?"

"People will find us," said Lily. She grinned. "We'll put out breadcrumbs for them, like Hansel and Gretel, and then when they find us, they'll get cake as a reward."

"Oh no," said Georgia, who had just heard the shop's doorbell ring. She looked sympathetically at June. "That's Mr Miniver. He's here already. He seems to be getting earlier every week."

Lily shook her head. "I don't understand how anybody who likes chocolate éclairs can be so inconsiderate."

In the distance, Mr Miniver and Sarah began to talk about the weather.[1]

June said, "Sometimes I wish I'd never met you all. Having to go back there after a day of this, it's…"

And then she did not say anything else because she could not.

"I'll go back instead of you," said Georgia instantly. "He'll never know. One schoolgirl is just the same as another to him."

"You could spend the week in the library and then come back next Saturday."

"Oh, can you *imagine* it?"

June took a deep breath. "We're not swapping," she said. "But thank you. Look—I'll bring the library to you.

---

1 This is something the British do as naturally as breathing.

That'll give me something to do. I'll borrow you one book every week and more than that if I can manage it."

Georgia's eyes lit up. She pushed Lily back and then when her sister did not move a satisfactory amount, climbed over her so that she was right next to June. "What? Are you serious? You'll really do that for me?"

June nodded. "You've all done so much for me." She felt a sudden and bright sense of purpose inside her heart. "Yes," she said. "Next week. When I come. I'll bring you something from the library, I promise. You can keep them for as long as you want. Nobody will mind." The school's library was an unloved space, thick with dust and sadness. June hadn't been into it for years. She hadn't even gone down the corridor it was in. But she would do it for Georgia.

"What if they want them back?" said Lily, in a squirming sort of manner from somewhere behind Georgia's elbow.

"They'll never notice," said June.

"I love you," said Georgia. "I'm so glad you ran away into our bakery."

And oh, how a part of me wants to stop this story there, but stories do not work that way.

They continue and so must this one.

Even though I do not wish it, it must.

LIKE A HOLE IN THE WORLD

June spent that week collecting books for Georgia. She volunteered to tidy out the maths cupboard and slid one of the books under her shirt before heading down to the library. Here she carefully selected a handful of books from the non-fiction shelf which she then hid under her blazer as well, before walking very gingerly back towards her dormitory. Luckily enough there was nobody else there, so she was able to disentangle herself from the books and carefully hide them in a bag under her bed. The bag would stay there until the end of the week when she would hand it to Georgia in person.

Mrs Parrish drove her into Little Hampden that Saturday and dropped her off at the end of the street. "Are you all right if I don't come all the way to the shop with you?" said Mrs Parrish. She barely looked at her. "It's just that I have a lot to do today and not very much time to do it in. Mr Miniver was meant to drop you off but then it all got very complicated and I got volunteered but I have to do all of these things and it's meant to be my day off—"

"It's okay," said June.

Mrs Parrish let out a sigh of relief. "I'll pick you up later from the bakery as normal. But you must promise me that you'll go straight there. Nowhere else."

"I promise," said June as she got out of the car. "I'll go straight to the bakery."

And so she did.

She walked down to the bakery, with her bag of books in one hand and a bouquet of flowers that she picked up in the florist as she passed in the other. They were destined for Sarah who had spent the last weekend being Very Tired in a way that had bothered June all week. It had felt like something more than the normal sort of tired that people got and so, she had picked up flowers for her in the hope that somehow they would make it better.

But when she got closer to the bakery, June realized that something was wrong.

The door of the bakery was closed. The lights were turned off.

And everything and everyone inside had gone.

THE GREATEST LIE

Silence.

Heavy, heavy silence.

Her own breath, coming from far away.

The flowers, suddenly too heavy to hold, falling to the floor.

Her body, standing still, unable to move for the entire day.

*

When Mrs Parrish came to pick her up, she said, "June, is everything okay?"

"Yes," said June. It was the greatest lie she had ever told. "It's fine."

THE WOMAN WHO LOOKED A LITTLE BIT LIKE A PENGUIN

June told that same lie to the other girls at school and she told it to Mr Miniver while he mourned the loss of his chocolate éclairs, and she told it to herself whenever she caught sight of her little blue notebook, still full of plans for the café. After a while, she could not bear to even look at that and went to the library. She placed the notebook on the first shelf that she came across and turned around and left it there and, after a while, forgot about it ever having existed in the first place.

That last part was another lie of course.

June did not forget any of it. She simply learnt to live with it.[1]

She lived with it during lunches full of kale soup and through every second of her final days at school. She lived with it when her parents told her that she could not come home when the school year ended because they were about to move house and there would be no room for her. And she lived with it even more when she

1   And that, my dear reader, is another lie as well.

folded up the letter that told her this and dropped it into the next bin that she saw.

On her final day at school, they were given speeches that were meant to inspire them for the future. One of these speeches was given by a woman who looked a little bit like a penguin. Her name was Good Sister Gladys and she was the head of the nuns who lived in the convent, just beyond the wood that surrounded the school. All of the other speakers had arrived at the school by car but she had arrived by helicopter and parked it on the playing fields. And because this was the 1950s and a time when women were not allowed to be remotely interesting, three members of staff had fainted in shock, while another two had handed in their resignations on the spot.

And all of this furore had resulted in June finally paying attention to what was happening before her.

Good Sister Gladys's speech was brief and to the point. She said, "I am very old and very wise and if I have learnt anything about life it is to make sure that you have your own toolbox," and then she sat down with a small and quite satisfied smile.

When the other[1] speeches were finished, the students were told to mingle with the speakers and learn Important And Life-Improving Things from them. June ignored all of this and instead went off to find Good Sister Gladys. She discovered her in the corner of the room, where

[1] Incredibly dull.

41

she was sitting by herself and eating a milk and honey biscuit.[1]

June said, "Hello," and, "I liked what you said," and neither of these sentences were good enough to express her feelings.

Good Sister Gladys smiled up at her. "Thank you. Biscuit?"

"Oh yes," said June. "Thank you."

And for a strange moment she felt as if Sarah Bishop was standing in front of her, about to rescue her all over again.

The two of them finished their biscuits in friendly silence before Good Sister Gladys said, "I'm supposed to ask you now about your future plans. At least, that's what your remarkably uninteresting headmaster said."

"I was going to be a baker," said June. "But then it got—complicated."

And for a moment, she was deeply impressed at how calm and in control she sounded.

"Perhaps a teacher then?" said Good Sister Gladys. She produced another two biscuits and gave one to June.

"I don't know," said June. "All of the teachers I've ever met didn't want to be anywhere near a classroom. I would have been sad about leaving if they had. But I'm not. I'm not sad at all." She paused then. "I just sometimes think

1 We do not have these now. They were sort of like a jammie dodger but instead of the jam, you had a tiny blob of honey surrounded by the cream filling. They were wonderful and I miss them intensely.

about what a place like this might be like if people actually wanted to be here. It could be everything and right now, I hate it. I've hated it for years. Sorry. I shouldn't be telling you any of this. Sorry. I didn't mean to bring it up."

It was strange, she thought, how some people could make you tell them everything.

"It's all right," said Good Sister Gladys. "Besides, if you can't tell the truth to a nun, then who else can you tell it to?"

June did not know what to say to that so she did not say anything at all.

When Good Sister Gladys finished her second biscuit, she stood up. "I have to go back to the convent now," she said. "But if you ever need a job, then you must come and see us. We value bakers most highly."

HOW TO COME HOME

And so, on her final day at school, June picked up her bag and walked through the wood and over the hill to where the convent stood and asked for a job in the kitchen there. She asked for it because she had nowhere else to go, and because the thought of hiding away from the world was all that she could think of, and because she rather thought Good Sister Gladys might understand all of this without her ever having to say it.

She got the job.

And when it came to the end of the day and the Good Sisters realized that she had nowhere to go home to, she got a room as well.

Within days June knew that she loved them all.

And within weeks, she decided to become a nun.

She made her vows to the order of the Good Sisters outside, underneath a full moon and a cold, sharp sky, and she felt the skin on the back of her neck tingle as she tucked her hair underneath the white scarf. The long black dress that she now had to wear went all the way down to her ankles and the sleeves touched the edge of her wrists. She had thought that she might feel ridiculous in it, or be unable to walk, but it felt right. All of it felt right.

It felt like home.

A BRIEF NOTE FROM
YOUR NARRATOR

At the start of this story, I promised you a nun who goes missing and three small girls who set out to bring her home. If you have been paying attention to the pages between there and here, then you will know that I have introduced you to a nun. Her name is June or, as she was known now, Good Sister June, and if you have been paying Especial Attention, you will know that she has not yet gone missing.[1] This is because you are a Smart Reader but also because we have Not Reached that time in the book yet.

And before we do, there are some other things that I need to tell you.

The first thing is this: bubbly white chocolate. It sounds like it should not work but it really definitely does. I recommend it entirely.

The second thing is this: June's old school had been in trouble. Although she had not realized it while she was there, the school had been losing money for years.

1 If you think she has already gone missing then I do not think you are paying attention. You should have a biscuit. It will help.

They had not recruited enough students to pay the bills or even half of them and so, sometime after June had moved to the convent and started her new life as a nun, the school closed down.

And the third thing that you need to know is this: Good Sister Gladys had a very good memory.

THE GOOD MEMORY OF
GOOD SISTER GLADYS

One morning at breakfast, almost a year to the day since Good Sister June had become a nun, Good Sister Gladys said, "Good Sister June, do you remember the first time we met? At your school?" She carefully began to spread her piece of toast with a thick layer of Fry's Chocolate Spread.[1]

"I remember it," said Good Sister June.

Good Sister Gladys nodded. She picked up her toast. "Did you know that they'd closed the school down now?" And out of the corner of her eye she gave Good Sister June a long and very specific kind of look.

"No," said Good Sister June, for she had not given the school another thought after her last day there and she had not gone anywhere near it since. She had already made herself forget the bakery and Georgia and Lily and Sarah. Forgetting her old school was nothing in comparison.

1 This was a type of chocolate spread that people ate in the 1950s. It was very perfect and sometimes I find myself dreaming about it even now.

"Do you remember what you said to me? The first time that we met?" asked Good Sister Gladys. She took a bite of her toast. "Perfect. But, alas, not enough chocolate." She put it back onto her plate to spread with a thicker layer of spread.[1]

Good Sister June nodded. "I remember. We talked about—I didn't know what I was going to do. We shared a biscuit. And then you offered me a job here."

"Really, I am *very* wise," said Good Sister Gladys. She took another bite of her toast and smiled with satisfaction. "Perfect. So. Was that all that we discussed on that day?"

"Yes," said Good Sister June and then, all of a sudden, she realized that it was not. They had mentioned the school. And how it could be different. About how it might be if people who wanted to be there were there.

She took a deep breath.

"I have an idea," she said.

"I rather thought you might," replied Good Sister Gladys.

---

1 This is one of the best things you can do with chocolate spread.

A SMALL PIECE OF PASTRY

Mr Charles Quinn of Quinn Solicitors[1] was very used to having a quiet life. He had served in the army during the war and when it had all ended, he had made himself two promises. He was going to have a quiet life and he was going to have an Eccles cake every day for his afternoon tea. An Eccles cake is not really a cake at all; it is a very small and crispy fruit pie pastry sort of thing, but Mr Quinn did not hold this against it at all. He was happy just to have one at four p.m. every day with a nice cup of coffee in his office when he could watch the world outside his office window.

One day, when he was approximately three bites in of his accustomed five, Mr Charles Quinn witnessed something rather unusual. There was a helicopter above the park opposite his window and it was lowering a small nun down onto the ground below. He watched with fascination as the nun purposefully cleared everybody out of the park before waving the helicopter down to land. Once the

1 A solicitor is a fancy word for somebody who handles legal and official things like "When is a cake not a cake in the eyes of the law?" (When it is ajar!) (Wait, that is the wrong punchline.) (Hang on, I cannot remember the right one.) (Clearly it is time for a biscuit.)

rotors had stilled, several more nuns climbed out of the helicopter. And then they all headed straight over the road and towards Mr Quinn's office.

This, as you might imagine, startled Mr Quinn entirely. He took the last two bites of his Eccles cake in a slightly too quick fashion and ended up getting a piece of pastry stuck inside his throat. He then tried to dislodge it by coughing but this only made things worse. At this point, his secretary knocked at the door and said, "There are some nuns here to see you." But he was coughing too much to reply.

This, as you might imagine, made his secretary even more concerned. She opened the door to check if he was all right and then stepped back as one of the nuns swept past her.

"Don't worry," said the nun, as she began to hit Mr Quinn on the back. "We're all trained in medical procedures."

And when all of this shocked the piece of pastry free from where it had been lodged, the breathless and red-eyed Mr Charles Quinn wondered if he had dreamt the whole affair.

"You're not dreaming," said one nun. "Frankly it's a good job we were here."

"We're trained in everything except heart bypasses," said one of the other nuns.

"But we're working on that," said another.

"Jolly good," he said faintly. He wiped his eyes. The nuns did not disappear.

"Time to focus, Mr Quinn," said the first nun. She had now, at last, stopped hitting him on the back. "My name is Good Sister Gladys, this is Good Sister June, this is Good Sister Paulette, and this is Good Sister Honey (who is very new to our family but makes excellent scones) and we are nuns from the local convent. We would like to buy that awful and abandoned school on the hill and turn it into the lovely school it was always meant to be, and we would like you to help us with this endeavour."

Mr Charles Quinn wiped his eyes again. He took another deep breath. The nuns still didn't disappear. In fact, there seemed to be more of them.

And he still had one bite of Eccles cake left.

"All right," he said, "Tell me what you need me to do."

INTRODUCING THE SCHOOL
OF THE GOOD SISTERS

And so Mr Charles Quinn of Quinn Solicitors helped the nuns to buy the awful school on the hill and transform it into the School of the Good Sisters, which was something rather beautiful indeed. There were not many pupils in those first few days because it took people a lot longer to find out about exciting things but they eventually did. More and more people began to send their daughters to the school because they knew that it offered them somewhere wonderful and somewhere good. The nuns did not teach their girls how to iron a shirt or how to make kale soup because they were too busy teaching them all of the important things instead. Their lessons were about things like how to fix a helicopter when all you had available was some macaroni and a wooden spoon; how to recite poetry in a brave and fearless fashion while riding upon a horse; and how to make the sort of friends that stayed with you for the rest of your life.

Good Sister Gladys was the first Headmistress of the School. She was half the size of the smallest girl there, did not hear half of the jokes that they told, and yet she was the centre of everything that happened. When she eventually decided to retire, she was replaced by Good Sister Sarah-Anne.[1] When Good Sister Sarah-Anne retired, she was replaced by Good Sister Margaret,[2] until eventually Good Sister June herself became the Headmistress.[3]

Being the Headmistress of the school meant that Good Sister June was responsible for everybody who lived inside it. This included the girls but also the other nuns, some of whom had been there ever since she had arrived at the convent all those years ago, and others who were as new and bouncy as the popcorn that Good Sister Honey gave out during their film nights.

The school looked after pupils aged twelve to eighteen, but anybody who was younger than that and needed to come to the school would always be found a space. It was a point of pride amongst the nuns that they never had, and would never, turn anybody away. The girls who were under twelve were known collectively as the first years and they were some of Good Sister June's absolute favourite people in the world.

[1] Here are three things about Good Sister Sarah-Anne: her favourite cake was lemon drizzle; she was the Headmistress who made midnight feasts part of the Official Curriculum; and she knew how to say, "Yes, I would quite like a biscuit, thank you," in fifteen different languages.
[2] Here are three things about Good Sister Margaret: she could never tell a joke without forgetting the punchline; her favourite cake was a chocolate sponge with extra icing; and she could give the sort of hugs that made you feel whole.
[3] And here is one thing that you need to know about Good Sister June: she is me.

When they were eighteen years old, the girls left school. Some of them went on to run entire countries and some of them came back to the school to teach, and some of them video called Good Sister Gwendolyn from the set of their movies in Hollywood.[1] Others began families of their own and, when their daughters were old enough, sent them to the school, while others became scientists who solved illnesses and brought hope to millions, and others still were very, very smart about things like ducks.[2]

The school is still based in the building that Good Sister Gladys and Mr Quinn purchased all those years ago. Sometimes Good Sister June could not quite understand how somewhere that was once so horrible could now be so wonderful. Yet whenever she did think like this, she found herself also feeling very happy that it was. No other girl would ever be as unhappy as she was here. She had made herself that promise a long time ago and was yet to break it.[3]

And in the next chapter, I am going to introduce you to one member of the School of the Good Sisters in particular.

1 For a while Good Sister Gwendolyn was convinced she was being haunted by a robot until one of the pupils told her that the frequent beeps from her pocket were, in fact, somebody trying to video call her.
2 By the way, do you know why ducks lay eggs? Because they would quack if they just dropped them.
3 One of the things that had helped with that promise was the fact that there were biscuits tucked away in every cupboard so neither nun nor girl was ever more than five metres away from an emergency custard cream.

Her name is Hanna Kowalczyk and she is—
Well.
She is everything.

INTRODUCING
HANNA KOWALCZYK

Hanna Kowalczyk has been described as being more book than person and I think that the person who described her like that is very clever indeed.[1] Hanna lived her life by books because they were the first thing that she ever understood. She would spend days by herself in the embassy[2] library trying to figure out what the words meant and then sounding them out one letter at a time. She never knew if she was pronouncing them properly because there was never anybody there to tell her. All she had were the stories but with them, she had everything.

The books that Hanna read told her what to do when you were stranded on a desert island with only a beautiful black stallion for company,[3] and how to put her name into

---

1 It was me.

2 An embassy is a little bit of a country that lives in another country. It is normally a big building full of people whose job it is to look after people from their country and to also share their culture and lives with the people from the country that they're living in.

3 This is a book called *The Black Stallion* by Walter Farley, and it is perfect.

the history book,[1] and even though many of these skills were not the sort of thing that could be often used in everyday life, Hanna knew that she would be ready for the extraordinary moment when they could.

The other important thing that you need to know about Hanna is this.

She was sent away to boarding school when she was only a handful of years old. This was something that happened to all of the children at her embassy and it was not because their parents did not love them, but rather because they lived complicated lives. They were diplomats and government officials who had to change homes and countries to be where and when their governments wanted them to be. Sometimes they would stay somewhere for months, other times it would just be for weeks, and more often than not it would just be for a few swift and frantic days. It was a life too unsettled for a small child and even though Marek and Gosia Kowalczyk tried to make it work for their quiet and owlish daughter, they knew that it was not going to work for long.

One day, when they received their assignments to go somewhere new, and they had only been where they were for a week, Marek and Gosia Kowalczyk looked at Hanna and knew that it was time for her to go to school. She needed to be somewhere safe and settled, somewhere

[1] This is from a book called *Ballet Shoes* by Noel Streatfeild. Her surname is pronounced "Strett-Field" and her books are almost as good as Victoria sponges.

that could understand her native Polish and teach her English so that she knew the language of the politicians and governments that Marek and Gosia worked with, and also be somewhere that she would not have to leave the moment that she got there. And when a friend in the embassy told them about a boarding school for girls that was deep in the English countryside and protected by nuns who knew both jiu-jitsu and how to ice a cupcake with their eyes closed, they thought that this might be somewhere that their beloved daughter might thrive.

And so they put Hanna on a plane and sent her away to school and even though their hearts broke a thousand times over when they did so, they told themselves that this was the right thing to do.

THE HEALING QUALITIES
OF A PINK WAFER

Over the years, Good Sister June had perfected a route through Little Hampden that did not go anywhere near the bakery. She knew that it was still there, of course, but she also knew that it would be becoming more and more of a shadow of the building that it once was. The paint would have faded, the shelves remained empty, and the cobwebs grown thicker. She did not wish to see any of it.

And so she had not let herself go anywhere near it, even when Good Sister Gladys had asked her to pick up the new girls from the village station. She had driven around the edges of the village and along deserted and long forgotten roads and when she eventually arrived at the station on the day that we join her, she had not thought about the bakery once.

She had thought about it much more than that.

But when she saw the girl at the station, who was already there and waiting for somebody to collect her, she realized that there was something much more immediate that she needed to think about. The girl was so pale and sad and still that she did not even look like a girl at all.

She looked like an outline that somebody had forgotten to colour in.

"Hello, Hanna," said Good Sister June. "My name is Good Sister June and I'm here to take you to the school." She repeated all of this in Polish, just to make sure that Hanna understood.

Hanna looked up. She opened her mouth to say something but no words came out. She could not even remember how to speak. Her whole body felt as if it wasn't hers any more. She had never felt anything like it.

Good Sister June rummaged into her bag and produced a biscuit. She gave it to Hanna. "Everything will be all right. Have a pink wafer."

IN WHICH GOOD SISTER JUNE FOLLOWS HER INSTINCT

There were many ways to introduce a new girl to the School of the Good Sisters and Good Sister June had done them all. Sometimes she would take the new child straight to their dormitory and introduce them to their new roommates, or if it had been at least thirty minutes since the child's last meal and they were consequently looking rather faint, she would take them to the kitchens where the gentle kindness of Good Sister Honey and the sweet taste of a freshly baked iced bun would tell the small and panicking soul that everything would be okay.

Some of the girls did not need help. They would march up the steps to the school themselves and they'd have the front door open before Good Sister June had even got out of the car. Other girls hung back and stared at the school for a long while until they could find the bravery to go inside. And then there were the other girls, who were so far gone in grief and sadness that they had almost forgotten how to live within the world. It was these girls who were handled the most gently of all and sometimes Good Sister June would sit with them outside the school for hours on end and only when the child was ready, would they eventually go inside.[1]

But on the day that Good Sister June returned to the school with Hanna, she did something that she had never done before.

She took the new girl straight to the school library.

And even though Hanna's English was not yet good enough to completely understand what Good Sister June was saying to her, nor even where she was taking her, when she saw the books and the soft glow of the sunlight on the shelves, she knew that she was home.

1 If you have read one of my books called *How To Be Brave*, then you will know that one of these girls was Elizabeth North. I shall not go over her story again but I shall tell you this: Elizabeth remains one of the bravest people that I have ever met.

HANNA'S FIRST
WEEK AT SCHOOL

For her first week, Hanna Kowalczyk lived and ate and slept within the library. She had not intended to do this but there was no need for her to leave it. She was a first year and one of the smallest first years in the school at the time and so her time was her own. All that the nuns wanted from her was the confidence to live her life on her own terms and for a long time, Hanna's confidence began and ended inside the library.

She understood the library. She loved it. Food always arrived at the library when she was hungry, and when she was sleepy, there was always a blanket to curl under and a sofa to sleep on. She read the books that she understood and then she started to work on the books that she did not. With these, she traced the letters and let them sink inside of her until all of a sudden, one day, she realized that she could understand them.

She found the biscuits that lived behind the picture books and the sticky marmalade cake that lived behind the fiction section and tucked into these as she read about tigers that came to tea and detectives solving crimes on the streets of Berlin. One night there was a storm and as the lightning flashed and the wind howled outside, she read about wild things throwing a wild rumpus and felt as if she was right there with them on their island.

She read all day and sometimes she read all night as well. One day she did not go to sleep because she was too busy reading a book about owl babies and having a Tiny Cry at the ending. She had never thought that boarding school might be as wonderful as this. She had never thought that *anything* could be as wonderful as this.

Hanna was not alone in the library of course. Sometimes Good Sister June would come and sit with her and tell her all about the secrets that she was yet to discover. She taught Hanna how to climb to the very top of the ladders so that she could reach the tins of toffees hidden at the tops of the twisting old shelves, and when it rained and the sky outside the window turned dark and grey, she taught Hanna how best to arrange the logs and firelighters inside the old fireplace to start a fire that made the library glow with light and warmth. On the days that it snowed and the trees in the wood beyond the school gates became covered in white, she took Hanna outside and helped her to hang lanterns from their branches before the two of them made snow angels on the freshly fallen snow. And when all of that was done, the two of them would talk about one hundred and one Dalmatians, little women and sheep-pigs until the sun rose up and a new day had begun.

There were other things, of course, that Good Sister June did not tell Hanna about and one of these things was a small blue notebook which had been written by a girl who once believed in dreams. But now, because she didn't, the notebook and all of the ideas for Bishop & Mortimer stayed on the highest shelf in the library, just where nobody could see it and where it could be forgotten.[1]

Sometimes Good Sister June and Hanna would be joined in the library by the other nuns. Good Sister Honey liked to get Hanna to test her new recipes and once that was done the three of them would colour code all of the bookshelves until another errand would call her away. Good Sister Paulette's visits were of a more practical nature and often ended up with Hanna helping her to rewire the lighting or change the fuses.[2] Good Sister Gwendolyn's visits were some of the best of them all because she was fond of pinning a white sheet against one of the bigger bookshelves and projecting classic movies for the three of them to watch in the evenings. Some of these films didn't have any sound at all and on these nights, Good Sister Robin would come and join them and provide her own soundtrack of Carefully Chosen But Quite Unmelodic Songs. To distract the others on those evenings, Good Sister Honey gave them tubs of sweet and salty popcorn and a tray full of freshly made

[1] Of course, at the end of this book everything is Quite Different and the notebook is held in pride of place in the— Hang on. I am not there yet and neither are you. Back up the page you go.
[2] "There is the slight risk of electrical shock," said Good Sister Paulette brightly. "But if you do get shocked, I will ensure you have extra pudding tonight to make up for it."

hotdogs, and on the side, in a small and quite unobtrusive manner, a box which contained several pairs of earplugs.[1]

And then, all of a sudden, Hanna decided to explore the world outside the library. It began when one morning, her feet turned towards the door and then before she quite realized what she was doing, she found herself pushing it open and walking out into the corridor. For the first time in several weeks, she was standing outside of the library and in the school itself. She could see classrooms full of girls in the distance, and hear the sounds of laughter and chatting from somewhere nearby, and then she spotted Good Sister June and walked over to join her as if she had been planning to do so all along.

"Hello, Hanna," said Good Sister June, looking down at her small duckling. "Do you want to join us?"

And to Hanna's intense and never-ending surprise, she did.

[1] "Just make sure you put the right things in your ears," said Good Sister Honey. "Because if you don't, then even I cannot help you."

FROM ONE WORLD
INTO THE NEXT

I would like to tell you that it was all as simple as that, but Hanna's newfound confidence was a half-formed, fragile thing. Every now and then it would completely disappear and she would find herself going back to the library to catch her breath, count to ten, and start all over again. The best part of those moments was that Good Sister June would always be there to greet her. She was never surprised to see Hanna and would never ask why she was back so early, but would just hand her a book or give her a slice of cake and let her do what she needed to do. This was to go to the darkest and most private corner of the library and stay there until her panic melted away and her confidence returned.[1]

After a while, Hanna began to realize that she was not alone. There were other girls in the school, some of them first years and some of them not, and all of them dealing

1 To find this place, you must turn left at *Five Children and It* and then go down the shelves until you reach *My Friend Flicka*. You must then look down to your left, just next to *Moominland Midwinter*, where you will see a small tunnel that leads into a tiny hole in the wall which is the perfect size for a hobbit or a very overwhelmed small girl.

with how best to tell their own stories in the world. She would see them creeping into the library beside her or picking up their own slice of cake from Good Sister June and then, all of a sudden, she'd find herself snuggling under a blanket on the sofa with the other girls and listening to one of the nuns read them a story about the Famous Five. One night, some of the older girls brought in marshmallows and showed Hanna how to toast them on the fire and then they ate them with sticky happiness while Good Sister Paulette told ghost stories.

And sometimes, when Good Sister June was not there, and Hanna still needed to do something to distract the soft and persistent anxiety inside her heart, she would put fresh flowers in all the vases and clean up all the tables and shelve all of the books. She found herself being helped in this by the tiniest and shyest of first years, some of whom were even smaller than her and still too nervous to speak in anything other than smiles. These were among Hanna's favourite visitors to the library and that was only a little bit influenced by the fact that they kept bringing in freshly baked moon cakes for her and leaving them behind the library desk.

And so it continued over the weeks and the months until one day, she was joined in the library by a girl called Edie Berger.

INTRODUCING EDIE BERGER

Here is what you need to know about Edie Berger.

If there is a revolution to be led, she will lead it. She is the daughter of activist parents who spend half their time protesting around the world and the rest of it in their family home in Paris, looking after the people who are nearest to them.[1] She is obsessed with macarons, hot chocolate made in the way that only French people can make it, staying in her bed until the very last moment possible, and having buttery scrambled eggs for breakfast. She can teach you how to make a barricade and what songs of revolutionary zeal you must sing upon it.

And when we join her in this chapter, she has been a pupil at the School of the Good Sisters for only three rather action-packed weeks.

She had not been convinced at first that she would like it at the school but after she had taste tested all of the French pâtisserie that Good Sister Honey had to offer and after Good Sister June had promised to add macarons to the menu on a regular basis, she had, at last, decided

---

1 If you would like to read more about this, then I wrote about it in a book called *How To Be True*.

to stay. She had announced this by posting a small notice on the front door of the school and then when this had not been noticed in the appropriate manner, posting a slightly bigger one and taking guided tours past it on the hour, every hour.

Edie had then begun to explore the school. As somebody who had lived in big houses all her life, she knew that they always had secrets about them. There would be a hidden door somewhere or a locked cupboard that nobody had opened for several hundreds of years. There might even be (and she was a little hazy about the details of this but still hopeful) pirate's treasure stored in a chest somewhere and just waiting to be found by a small and rather brilliant French girl.

She had found paintings of women whose eyes seemed to watch her as she walked past them, tall towers with windows that were mysteriously invisible when she went outside to look for them, and a whole network of corridors hidden between the walls that slid in and around all of the official rooms that everybody else seemed to know.[1] She had hidden Emergency Biscuits underneath one of the floorboards in Good Sister June's office,[2] a pack of

[1] And this, perhaps, was the greatest discovery of all because that meant that Edie could get around the school within minutes without anybody knowing how she was doing it. It was a talent that had come in very useful in another book I wrote called *How To Be Brave*.

[2] Should anybody tell you that Good Sister June accidentally on purpose ate them, you must tell them that you completely understand why she did that and that it was No Accident and really she is not to blame at all.

Emergency Dried Sausage behind one of the cupboards in the fifth form common room,[1] and three Tins of Emergency Cassoulet, all lined up like soldiers, behind the statue of Good Sister Gladys on the top floor. Edie was not completely sure what all these emergencies were but she was also somebody who wanted to be ready for anything that might come her way.

When she had finished her preparations, Edie Berger realized something very particular about the world.

Biscuits and *cassoulet* and *charcuterie* were all very good, but they were better with a friend.

And so she was going to find one.

---

1 You should not get dear Edie onto the topic of *charcuterie* because, if you do, you will be there for many, many hours. Alas, I speak from experience.

EDIE BERGER'S VERY SPECIFIC LIST OF FRIENDSHIP REQUIREMENTS

I am going to place these in bullet points because I am very helpful and also because I accidentally changed the little bullet points to pictures of a Victoria sponge and now I can't change them back. Also, if I am honest, I am not sure that I want to because I find them Quite Inspirational like that.

- Edie's friend must be able to support her in all of her exploits, both legal and otherwise, and not panic when things go awry.
- Her friend must appreciate the very precise joy of a macaron but not as much as Edie herself because that would only create drama around the afternoon tea table.
- They must be able to make emergency sandwiches with the crust cut off, and also be able to make these in severe and potentially life-threatening circumstances.
- They must be ready to embrace adventure with all their heart.

I THINK THIS IS THE BEGINNING OF A BEAUTIFUL FRIENDSHIP

Every library is magical at midnight and the library at the School of the Good Sisters was no exception. Hanna had opened all the windows and pulled back the curtains and several groups of girls had gathered right in front of them to build book forts in the moonlight. In the far corner of the room, Good Sister Gwendolyn was introducing the cinema club to *Singin' in the Rain*[1] while another group of girls were sitting around a table and were happily testing Good Sister Honey's new recipe for chocolate gingerbread brownies.[2] Several of the smallest girls were wrapped up in blankets and gently snoozing on some of the comfiest chairs, whilst those who were still awake were listening to Hanna read to them from *The Borrowers*.

Edie waited until the last small member of Hanna's audience had closed their eyes and begun to snore before

---

1 There is singing, there is dancing, and there is a Very Important Cake and if this doesn't make it the best film in the entire world, then I do not know what does.

2 The secret is this: when you think you have enough icing, you must put on some more.

she headed over to join her. For a moment, the two girls studied each other before Edie spoke.

"Hello," she said. "My name is Edmée Agathe Aurore Berger. It is a lot, I know, but also, I *am* French. However! Enough about me. Are you Hanna Kowalczyk?"

"Yes," said Hanna.

"Tell me, what is your opinion on macarons?"

"I like them," said Hanna.

"One last question," said Edie. "If there is a cupcake that is iced most perfectly with chocolate icing, and a cupcake that is iced in a similarly quite perfect style with kale icing, which would you choose?"

"Chocolate," said Hanna, for this was not a question in the slightest.

"Perfect," said Edie. "Then we will be the very best of friends."

And that was how it all began.

AND CALLA MAKES THREE

The friendship of Hanna Kowalczyk and Edie Berger was like cheese on toast: the two of them made each other better in ways that nobody could have ever imagined. Hanna helped Edie to feel at home in the school, while Edie helped Hanna come out of the last little bits of her shell.[1]

But it was not a complete sort of friendship until they met their third.

And she was a girl called Calla North.

Calla is the daughter of Elizabeth North, the world's leading expert on ducks, and so Calla has some very specific knowledge about the world. She knows what a duck does when it is unwell,[2] why ducks love Christmas,[3] and what a duck's favourite television programme is.[4] Elizabeth and Calla lived a very difficult life for a very long time until the world finally gave them a chance to survive. Calla's first term at the School of the Good

---

1 A metaphorical shell and not a real life one.
2 They phone the ducktor.
3 Because they get to pull quackers.
4 A duckumentary.

Sisters was not the most normal of first terms[1] but with the help of Hanna and Edie and all of their friends, she came through it in one piece.

Calla is very fond of ice cream and will eat any flavour if it has sprinkles and a chocolate flake on top. Her favourite biscuit is a white chocolate wafer, her favourite sandwich filling is chips with extra salt and ketchup, and she knows that all of this tastes better when eaten at the seaside on a bright-blue-sky sort of day. She is also very good at being organized and looking after people and when she is not looking after her mum or Edie or Hanna, she keeps an eye on our more chaotic first years.[2]

Family is very important to Calla. For a long while it was just her and her mother because her father died when she was very young. Sometimes, when she is at home, Calla will go and spend the whole day by his grave and update him on all the news. Some people might think this is strange but I think it is rather wonderful. Why on earth would you not want to keep talking to the people that you love?

When she came to school, Calla met Good Sister June and Good Sister Christine,[3] and then she met Edie and Hanna, and then all of their friends and then all of their friends' friends and somewhere in the middle of all of this, she realized that it wasn't just her and her mum against

1 Trust me, a *lot* happened.
2 I must admit that many of the first years do fall into this category and so our dear Calla is kept quite busy most of the time.
3 Who was Elizabeth's childhood best friend.

all of the world. Her family had grown a thousand times over and all of these people around her felt like armour.

And a little part of her, which was happier than she had ever thought possible, knew that she would never let it or them go.

BACK IN THE PRESENT DAY

It is time for us to jump forward several years to the start of a new term and to Hanna, Calla and Edie, travelling back from their school holidays in Switzerland. They had been with Edie's grandmothers and eaten an enormous quantity of dumplings and potato rösti that had been so good that Edie had crowned herself the Queen of the Potato and insisted on there being an Official Ceremony and three days of feasting.

On the last day of the holidays, they were meant to be picked up by Hanna's parents. Marek and Gosia Kowalczyk had been living in Europe for several months at that point and had offered to drive the girls back to school. Hanna had not quite believed it when they told her and then on that last day, she believed it just a little bit less.

Because her parents did not come. They were called away at the last moment and so they sent a young member of staff from the embassy instead with their apology for Hanna. It was an apology that she listened to but did not hear a single word of. Calla and Edie realized that something was not right, for they were her very best of friends, but she told them that she was fine and to get in the car. It was a lie, of course, but it was the only way she could keep herself together at that point.

And so the three of them began their journey back to school, and as the miles went by and Calla and Edie discussed whether they were distantly related to royalty[1] or how best to say hello to a talking duck,[2] Hanna pushed her sadness far away from her. It was just another day in her life, she told herself, and her parents weren't to blame for how it had turned out. They were busy people. They led busy lives. It was never going to work. Being normal and present and standing at her side was something that they could not do. It was impossible. Sometimes she forgot that. Today had just reminded her. That was it. That was all it was ever going to be.

And this is what she told herself as Edie parked the car on the ferry[3] and she told herself again as they sat on the top deck to eat their ferry biscuits[4] and she told herself again and again as the coast of France faded into the distance, and every time she told herself, she believed it a little bit more.

---

1 Edie, suspiciously: "I think the King of England is *very* French."
2 Calla, knowledgeably: "The same way you'd say hello to *any* duck."
3 Their driver, whose name was Andrej: "I can't park it in that tiny space."
Edie, taking the wheel: "I can."
4 Ferry biscuits are sock biscuits that are meant to be eaten only when you get on a ferry. Sock biscuits are biscuits that live in your sock. Socks are the things you put on your feet before you put your shoes on. A shoe? Bless you!

THE FIRST DAY OF TERM

They arrived at the School of the Good Sisters late that same afternoon, and the first out of the car was Calla. She had a packet of chocolate biscuits in one hand and her phone in the other. She recorded a quick message for her mother before being distracted by Eloise Taylor, who had chosen this particular moment to dangle off the South Tower roof. The only problem was that she was not really dangling but was actually sort of stuck and slightly in need of rescuing. Calla was both somebody tall enough to help and somebody who also had biscuits, and so was currently in the process of being surrounded by first years and asked to help.

The second girl out of the car was Edie, who had balanced a crown[1] on top of her wild curls. The moment that her feet touched the ground, she announced in a loud voice, "I AM BACK AND I HAVE BROUGHT A NEW RECIPE FOR DUMPLINGS," which made several small first years promptly faint from over-excitement. Edie gave the first years that were still vertical an approving smile before heading off purposefully into the building.

---

1 Which had written on it: "Queen Of The Rösti".

The last girl in the car, Hanna, got out in a slightly more awkward fashion. This was because she was both getting out of the car but also turning back to check on Andrej's whereabouts. He had been carefully unloading their luggage throughout all of this and piling it up against the tree.

"My God," he said, grunting with effort, "is there a dead body in this one?"

"That's Edie's bag," said Hanna, "so perhaps there is, yes."

"Talking of your friends, where have they gone?"

Hanna studied the courtyard. It was full of girls but neither Calla nor Edie were anywhere to be seen. Neither, she suddenly realized, was Good Sister June. "I don't know. Maybe they're all inside."

"Well, you cannot carry these bags inside by yourself. I will help you."

"Oh no, you don't have to," said Hanna. "I'll sort them out. You need to get to the ferry and back. The traffic might be bad."

"Are you sure?"

"Yes," she said.

"Do you want me to give your parents a message from you or anything?"

And here Hanna paused for a long, long moment.

"Tell them I'm fine," she said. "Tell them that."

COMING HOME

Hanna took all of the bags up to the North Tower bedroom and when she was done, she made her way back down the stairs and headed off to a very particular place. This was Good Sister June's office and it was the very heart of the entire school. The corridor walls leading up to it had been covered in brightly coloured handprints from all of the girls who had studied at the school before and the door itself was freshly painted at the start of every term. On this day in particular, it had been painted in a yellow that made Hanna think of scrambled eggs and custard tarts. She took a moment to appreciate this before she knocked twice on the door and waited for Good Sister June to invite her in.

After a while, when there was no response, Hanna said, "Hello?" and pushed open the door. She had done this a thousand times before and knew what she *should* see inside the room. There should be shelves full of afternoon tea china, and another one piled high with biscuit tins and cake tubs. Next to these would be a row of cake stands of varying sizes so that there was always a cake big enough for everybody to get a slice of it, and behind these was a collection of tins and boxes full of biscuits and toffees and boiled sweets suitable for every emergency. And Good Sister June herself, right there in the middle of it.

But the room was deserted. There was no sign of Good Sister June anywhere.

Hanna stood there for a long moment. It was the first time in years that Good Sister June had not been present at the start of term. She was always there. Everybody knew it. She would talk to the new parents and the shy, wobbly new girls and every now and then she would be disturbed by the returning girls who would run in and wave a hello or wrap their arms around her before heading off to start the new term. And now she was nowhere to be seen.

"It is quite possible she is somewhere else," said Hanna out loud. This was not for the benefit of anybody listening[1] but rather for the benefit of the slightly uncomfortable sensation inside of her stomach. It was a sensation that required the prompt finding of Good Sister June to resolve and so she set off to do precisely that.

She checked inside all of the classrooms and behind the backs of all the sofas and, remembering one of her favourite books,[2] even looked inside the piano in the music room. She checked the laboratories on the third floor and tried not to be distracted by the smells of the barbecue that was being set up on the fourth. On the fifth floor, she ignored something that sounded remarkably like a

---

[1] For as we have just established there was nobody else there.
[2] *Jo of the Chalet School* by Elinor M. Brent-Dyer

concrete mixer starting to rumble and the soft slap of somebody spooning material into it,[1] and on the sixth, she leant out of a window to make sure that Good Sister June had not appeared outside while she had been looking for her. The yard was full of cars and buses and there were girls everywhere. Some of them were on top of the buses and some of them dangling off trees and every minute that passed brought more of them.

But still no Good Sister June.

And so Hanna took a deep breath and went to check the library.

[1] That somebody's name rhymed with Schmedie Schmerger.

A SPECIAL KIND OF MAGIC

"**G**ood Sister June? Are you in here?"

But there was no one there and definitely not a missing nun.

Hanna took a moment to be completely sure. She checked behind the books on the top shelf and then on the bottom as well. She opened all the curtains and looked underneath the issues desk and if all that was not enough, she even checked inside the tiny little hole that she had hidden in herself, all of those years ago.

And still Good Sister June was nowhere to be found.

The little feeling of unease inside of Hanna's stomach began to grow.

It was only when she reached the far corner of the library that Hanna realized something was different. One of the tables, just underneath the last window that looked out on to the trees, was covered in newspapers and books. The chair had been pushed out, as if somebody had left in a hurry, and in the middle of the table was a small and dusty notebook. Hanna picked this up out of interest and started to look through it. She knew all of the books in the library and this was something brand new to her. And yet the dust on its cover suggested that it had been wherever it had been for quite some time.[1]

It all grew even stranger when she realized that the notebook was full of ideas for a café.[2]

"Welcome to the Bishop and Mortimer Book-Café," said Hanna, reading the title page out loud. She began to turn the pages. One of them had a detailed recipe for Victoria sponge written on it in oddly familiar writing. Next to it was a design for a café sign, and on the page opposite was a list of ingredients ranked in order of deliciousness. Every page had something different on it. One had a list of cookery books while another had drawings of the best chairs for people to sit on and yet another had ideas for afternoon tea sandwiches. There were even lists of villages and places marked as potential locations.

But then, all of a sudden, it all stopped and the pages turned empty.

Hanna put the notebook back down on the table and studied the rest of the mess thoughtfully. None of it made sense. The dates on the newspapers were from the past few weeks so that suggested that one of the nuns had probably been reading them. The girls had only just got back today, after all. But if it was one of the nuns who had been in here, then something must have happened to stop them from tidying up after themselves.

---

1 Indeed it had. And yet it had felt like only minutes had passed for the person who had put it up there.
2 Sound familiar?

This all seemed like it had been abandoned and done so in a rush.

In the distance she heard a flurry of girls run down the corridor. She glanced at the clock. It was almost time for tea.

And still, she thought, she had not found her head-mistress.

GOING INSIDE THE WALL

The next place that Hanna decided to look was not technically a place at all.

She headed down the corridor away from the library. She took a left at a shelf full of baked beans, turned right at the Emergency Custard Cream cupboard, before finally coming to a halt in front of a nondescript wall that nobody else in the entire school ever stopped at. This was because the wallpaper had faded in the sunlight and where it had not faded, it had started to peel in long ribbons down the wall. It was the sort of wall that should have been redecorated and looked after but that would have required it being noticed and nobody ever really had.

Except one girl.

Her name was Edie Berger.

And the first person she had shared her discovery with was her best friend.

Hanna looked left and right and then left and right again until she was completely satisfied that she was not being watched.

And then she pressed firmly on a very particular part of the wall.

The wood creaked; in the distance, levers shifted, and all of a sudden the wall opened up in front of her.

And Hanna stepped inside it.

Not every building has a world between the walls but the School of the Good Sisters does. It is the kind of building that looks normal the first time you see it but the second time you look, you start to see all the ways that it is not. There is a window, for example, on the fourth floor to a room that nobody has ever been able to find their way into[1] and a tower on the fifth that has an extra tower built on top of it as if somebody had got very good at building towers and did not know how to stop. The rest of the roof is flat and perfect for a midnight feast but every now and then there are tiny extra roofs poking out from the side as if somebody began to ice a cake and could not stop themselves from adding more bits when they were done.

Hanna was one of only a handful of girls in the school, and an even smaller handful of nuns, who knew about the world between the walls. She and her friends could get from one side of the school to the other and back again before anybody would have noticed she'd even gone anywhere in the first place and when circumstances had required it of her, she had attended secret meetings and midnight feasts and also witnessed people win hide-and-seek in a Most Convincing Fashion.[2]

---

1 We have looked for several years but never been successful.
2 This was Amelie Stansfield, who stayed between the walls for three weeks and only emerged when Good Sister Honey lured her out with the smell of a freshly baked marble cake.

On this day in particular, she checked all of the big rooms that were inside of the walls and all of the small ones as well. She climbed the ladders up to the long corridors on the fifth floor, and down into the cellars that ran beneath the tennis court before heading to the school kitchens. Here she paused to peer into the kitchens where she saw Good Sister Honey happily icing a triple decker sponge cake and, rather strangely, an enormous shadow of a man standing in the doorway. She could not see who it was but she knew, quite clearly, that it was not Good Sister June and so she continued in her search.

She only paused in her endeavours when she came across Edie coming down from one of the attics. Her friend was carrying a small plate of olives and pausing every other step to carefully nibble one before she continued.

"Hello," said Hanna. "I thought I heard a concrete mixer going earlier. Was that you?"

"You *did* and it *was*," replied Edie happily. "I have paused only to acquire sustenance before returning to it."

"Have you seen Good Sister June anywhere?"

Edie looked thoughtful. "She was not where I have been but I have not been everywhere yet. For example, I am yet to visit South America to try the *Torta Negra Galesa* and—"

But this sentence must remain unfinished because Hanna had already left.

LIKE AN ACHE IN
THE STOMACH THAT
WON'T GO AWAY

The final place that Hanna checked was the front yard and she stayed there until the last vehicle had been and gone. This was a taxi which unloaded three small and quite overwhelmed new girls who looked so startled by what lay before them that they did not move. And when she saw this, Hanna put her worries about Good Sister June to the side and headed down to tell them that it was all going to be okay. Good Sister Honey, however, got there first. She whisked the girls down to the kitchen for a sustaining plate full of sausages and roast potatoes. Only when they had finished that, did she show them to their bedrooms and introduce them to the other first years.[1]

And it was when Good Sister Honey bore off her charges that Hanna finally understood that Good Sister June was not here either. She took a deep breath and

[1] You may be interested to know that the first years were having a welcome-back-to-school-who-has-cake-let's-eat-it party and that is the sort of situation that nobody could be scared of even if they tried.

headed inside the school and up to the North Tower bedroom. When she opened the door, Calla looked up.

"Hanna! Where have you been? I'm so sorry I disappeared! I didn't mean to leave you by yourself but Lily Maguire wanted to ask me about the unusual pond that had formed outside her bedroom window and I said, 'Well it can't be a pond, can it, Lily, because it is in *mid-air*,' and then it turned out that the pond was just Sally Campbell who is excellent at camouflage skills and—"

"Have you seen Good Sister June?" said Hanna.

"No," said Calla. She paused for a moment to think. "Actually, I don't think I've seen her since we got back."

"Don't you think that's strange?"

"Did you check the library?"

Hanna gave Calla a very long and very hard stare.

Calla stuck her hands up in apology. "Sorry," she said, "go on."

"I checked the study and I checked the library and I checked all the classrooms and then between the walls and then I went outside and there was nobody there and I waited until everybody was back and I haven't found Good Sister June anywhere."

"Oh, Hanna," said Calla very gently. "She'll be somewhere."

"But she isn't," said Hanna. "She isn't anywhere and that's the point." And then, in a very different tone of voice, she said, "Hang on. There's something at the window."

AN EDIE BERGER SORT
OF SOMETHING

Hanna crossed the room and leant out of the window. She twisted so that she was looking up towards the top of the tower where her other best friend was currently dangling. Her legs were hanging off the side of the roof while her hands were fixing a bundle of wires and a metallic box to the very top of the tower.

"What are you doing and is it legal?" asked Hanna, with the wisdom born of a very long friendship.

"I am affixing a radio receiver to our tower so we can intercept traffic between all of the key intelligence agencies and also the communications from a man called Malcolm who lives in Hampstead and *thinks* he is undercover but really he is not," said Edie.

Hanna narrowed her eyes. "What happened to the concrete mixer?"

"Oh, I have plans for that as well," said Edie. "Let us just say that they involve a water pistol, several slices of Victoria sponge and, if all goes well, a spatula." She twisted the last roll of wire around the top of the tower, secured it with a pair of pliers that she produced from somewhere deep inside her hair, before swinging herself in through the bedroom window. Within three steps she was in front of them, her hands on her hips and her eyes bright with interest. "So!" she said, "Why do you both look so serious?"

"I haven't found Good Sister June," said Hanna.

"Not even after you left me?"

Hanna shook her head.

"Are you, perhaps, having an instinct?" said Edie. "Do you feel as if you have too much and also too little? Is your tummy tingling like you have got goose pimples on the inside? Do your feet itch with the sensation of adventure?"

"Yes," said Hanna.

"Have you eaten?"

"No," said Hanna.

"Then the first place that we will search for Good Sister June is at dinner," said Edie in a purposeful fashion. "And she will be there because it is the first night of term and Good Sister Honey's menu choices are always remarkable on such an occasion and nobody, but nobody, would ever miss such an occasion. All you need to do, my little Hanna banana bread, is quiet your instinct just for an hour or two and then, when Good Sister June is sitting at the staff table, tell yourself that it is all going to be okay. Of course, if she is not there, then we act on your instinct and begin an adventure on our satisfyingly full stomachs."

"Am I dreaming or did some of that actually just make sense?" said Calla.

"I think it did," said Hanna.

"I always make sense," said Edie with great dignity. "The only problem is that neither of you are French enough to see it."

POTATOES AT DAWN

Hanna had spent many first nights in the School of the Good Sisters but they had never been quite like this. Even though the hall was covered in bunting which ran from corner to corner,[1] and each table was full of fresh flowers and bowls full of emergency scones to snack on, none of this mattered because Good Sister June was nowhere to be seen or heard and not one nun had mentioned anything about it. They were all sitting at the staff table and firmly ignoring all of the enquiring glances being sent their way.

"Oh, they are HIDING something," said Edie, who had spent her last five potatoes staring at Good Sister Christine in a pointed fashion. "Your instinct was quite right, Hanna, my dear little pasta salad. Something is wrong and I think that it all centres on the fact that our beloved Headmistress is nowhere to be seen." At this point she swung around to give Calla a quick grin. "At least it does not look like the sort of something that has resulted in an evil headmistress who is here to kidnap you and that is a PLUS, is it not?"

---

1 And in one rather remarkable circle in the middle where Good Sister Gwendolyn had got a little bit lost.

"It is indeed," said Calla. "One kidnapping attempt is enough for me, thank you."

Edie nodded and then leant over her to address the other girls sitting at the table. "My friends, my chums and even you, Rose Bastable! Your attention, please! I would prepare yourselves, for a mystery is afoot and it will fall to us to solve it. Do your stretches! Refresh yourselves on your covert skills! Eat all of your dinner and ask for seconds because *none* of us can do anything on empty stomachs and anybody who demands otherwise is a monster and must be ignored with all our souls!"

"I'm going to go and talk to Good Sister Christine," said Hanna.

Calla grabbed her arm. "I know you're worried," she said, "but hang on for a moment. Good Sister Christine is lovely and wonderful in a thousand different ways but she's still a grown-up and she will not tell you anything when everyone's looking at her. She might even *explode*."

"I'm not sure she'll explode," said Rose Bastable, as she leant over to steal Edie's last potato.

"She might," said Edie, as she stole her potato right back. "But! No! Enough! We shall continue this discussion later for Good Sister Christine is about to say something useful, and it is the sort of useful that, I think, is going to have a chapter all of its own."

A CHAPTER ALL OF ITS OWN

"**H**ello, everyone. My name is Good Sister Christine and I would like to welcome you to a new term at the School of the Good Sisters. And if this is your first term with us, you are most welcome. The next few days may feel a little bit scary or confusing but I promise you that, all of a sudden, they will not be. Trust me, I know this from experience. Many hundreds of years ago I was a pupil, just like you. I joined when I was very little and then, as you can tell, never left. I made the best friend of my life here and we're still friends now."

At this point, Good Sister Christine caught Calla's eye and gave her a quick smile because her best friend was Calla's mother, Elizabeth, and the friendship between the two of them was one of the most wonderful things in her life.

But even as Calla smiled back at her, Hanna could not help noticing that Good Sister Christine's smile was not as wide as it normally was.

"Being here means that you're part of a family," continued Good Sister Christine, turning her attention back to the room. "We are the School of the Good Sisters and wherever you go in the world, you will always be part of our family. That means that you must look after the people who need looking after, and always stand up for the people who need standing up for, and always—but always—make sure that you stop everything in time for afternoon tea."

A sudden tear sparked in Edie's eye at this. She wiped it away. "Beautiful."

Good Sister Christine took a deep breath. "Many of you might be wondering why I am the one giving this speech. Normally it's the responsibility of the Headmistress and *normally* I am not her."

Hanna leant forward on her elbows.

"But today I am," said Good Sister Christine. "I am standing in for Good Sister June, who has... gone on holiday... and so this term, I am your Headmistress. That means that I am going to be the one who is in charge of everything and—"

I do hope that Good Sister Christine does not mind me cutting her off here, because the rest of her speech really was very good, but this is the point at which almost the entire school had stopped listening. This was because the thought of an entire term without Good Sister June was almost incomprehensible, but for the three girls of the North Tower bedroom, it was something more.

Edie looked at Calla and then the two of them looked directly at Hanna.

Hanna shook her head. "That woman is not telling the truth."

Lies could be told everywhere else, but not here and not by Good Sister Christine or the other nuns.

And she had trusted all of them completely, ever since she had arrived at the school.

Until today.

Until now.

IN WHICH, A MOMENT
PRESENTS ITSELF

The thing that I must now tell you is this: good people do not tell their lies from choice. There is always a reason behind such lies and sometimes it can be good and sometimes it can be bad, but there is always something behind them. And one of the most interesting things that you can do when you realize that somebody is lying to you is try to work out what that something is.[1]

It was because of this that Hanna and Calla and Edie did not do anything.

At least, not immediately.

They just made sure that they were the last three people to finish their main course and that they were the last three people to finish their desserts as well.

This did not go unnoticed. Rose Bastable tried to take Edie's temperature and was only distracted when Sally Campbell laid a trail of custard creams in the opposite direction. Several of the first years were only persuaded

---

1 Obviously this can be a tiny bit difficult if the person has told you a mean or nasty lie but then one of the things that you can do is to ignore them completely and go and find somebody nice to share your cake with instead.

that they did not need to provide pink wafers to make Calla smile once more when Lucy Millais and Maisie Holloway invited them to an impromptu fish finger banquet in their common room. And Hanna's small band of loyal readers were only persuaded not to besiege their idol with reading suggestions by the sudden request of Jia Liu and Eloise Taylor for help in building a book fort.

And so, when all of the other nuns had gone, and all of the other girls had gone, and Edie had finally placed all of the leftover roast potatoes in her emergency leftover roast potato tub, the three girls and Good Sister Christine were finally alone.

"All right, you three," said Good Sister Christine. "What's going on?"

Hanna, Edie and Calla smiled up at her in a very innocent manner.

"Well, if I didn't suspect it, now I know that something's going on," said Good Sister Christine in a resigned fashion. She leant back on the nearest table and folded her arms. "You've not even been back a day and you're already plotting something."

"We are not plotting anything," said Edie, who was rather enjoying telling the truth. They hadn't plotted anything. Yet. "We are just good and obedient pupils who would like to have a tiny discussion with you about unimportant things!"

Hanna watched a small smile cross Good Sister Christine's face and a little bit of her heart warmed at the sight of it. Even though Good Sister Christine was not telling them the truth about Good Sister June's absence, it seemed that she might still be her old self underneath it. The self that would answer questions when asked. And actually tell the truth.

So she decided to test her theory.

"Where's Good Sister June—really?"

And when Good Sister Christine did not immediately answer, Hanna knew that there was something very much up indeed.

THE NOBLE CODE
OF LIBRARIANS

"I can't tell you," said Good Sister Christine.

"Yes, you can," said Hanna.

The two of them narrowed their eyes at each other.

Edie's head swivelled from left to right.

Calla made a small and very British sound of awkwardness.

And Hanna felt very, very uncomfortable until she realized that if she had been the one who was missing, then Good Sister June would have moved heaven and earth to find her. That was what family did. That was what *she* had to do right now.

So she took a deep breath and continued.

"There's something going on with Good Sister June. She wouldn't just disappear without an explanation. And right now, it looks like she's done exactly that. I need to know what you know."

Good Sister Christine sighed. "Hanna, we can't talk about it. You need to let the adults handle this."

"Not *you* mentioning adults," said Hanna, appalled. "Good Sister Christine, I never thought you'd talk to me like this."

"Hanna, I'm not doing it on purpose. There's just a lot of things going on right now. All of the stuff with the governors for one, and with that man.[1] I just don't want to—I can't tell you about it. I would if I could but I can't."

"But you could," replied Hanna. "You're a *librarian*. You helped me with the secret library when that horrible other Headmistress was here, and the sort of person who runs a Forbidden Library believes in doing the right thing. At least, that's what I thought."

Edie stepped back.

Calla stepped back.

But Good Sister Christine didn't move an inch.

And neither did Hanna. "Good Sister June is missing and everything feels weird and you are not telling us the truth."

It was then that, all of a sudden, Good Sister Christine said something rather unexpected. "She's gone."

Hanna took a step back. "She's—what?"

"She's gone," repeated Good Sister Christine. "She didn't say goodbye. She disappeared about a week ago. We woke up, and she was just gone. And we don't know when or even if she's coming back."

And when she said that, Hanna heard nothing but the sound of drums in her ears.

"But that just doesn't sound like her," said Calla blankly. "I know sometimes my mum would get so excited about some new piece of research that she'd just go out of the

---

1 Remember this, it's important.

house and never say a word, but she'd always leave me a note to say where she'd gone."

Good Sister Christine reached into her pocket. "I have a note," she said. "She pushed it under my bedroom door before she went wherever she's gone. I almost didn't see it."

"May we read it, my dear Good Sister Christine?" said Edie gently. "I know that it might be personal and I understand if it is, but if you can, then I think it might help us to see it. You know how much we care for her. How much she means to all of us."

For a moment Good Sister Christine held the note in her hand.

And then she handed it over.

THE NOTE

Dearest Chrissie.

When you wake up, I will be gone. I don't know when I'll be back. I don't know even if I'll be back. Don't look for me. I have to do this by myself. I have to find somebody before it's too late. I've already taken too long.

Take care of the school. You're in charge now. You'll be wonderful.

I'm sorry. I really am so very sorry.

June

KEEPING UP APPEARANCES

When Calla had finished reading the note out loud, Hanna had the strangest sensation that she wasn't in the room any more. She was in the library instead and Good Sister June was in front of her, pulling her towards a particular shelf. "Try this one," she said, pointing at a copy of *Eustacia Goes to the Chalet School*. "It's a bit dramatic at times but it ends well. Books like this always do."

"Hanna," said Edie, breaking through her thoughts. "Are you all right?"

"Yes," said Hanna, still with the memory of Good Sister June at her side and the weight of the book in her hands. She blinked and made herself focus on the room and the matter at hand. "Good Sister Christine, what was Good Sister June like the last time you spoke to her? Something like this doesn't come out of nowhere. There has to be something else going on here."

"If I knew, then I'd tell you," said Good Sister Christine. "All I can say is that when I last saw her, she was really upset. She wouldn't tell me anything but I knew that there was something wrong. I mean, we had a freshly baked Victoria sponge for afternoon tea and she only took one slice."

"*Mon dieu*," said Edie.

"I know," said Good Sister Christine. She scrubbed her hand across her eyes. "She said that she had a headache and then she went to bed, but her bed wasn't slept in. She just left. And she won't have taken a phone because she doesn't have one except for the landline in her office, and the only thing keeping me from going after her myself is the fact that I have to run the school and look after all of you."

"So we'll go," said Hanna suddenly. "We'll go and find Good Sister June and bring her home."

"You will not," said Good Sister Christine. "Girls, normally I would allow and encourage this sort of thing but I'm responsible for you now. I'm your Headmistress. I have to think about that."

Edie stared at her with shock.

Calla said, "Good Sister Christine, what are you saying?"

"This is me being the adult," said Good Sister Christine. She did not look particularly happy about it. "I'm not happy about it but there we are. I'm sorry but I can't let you just go off by yourselves. I won't allow it. Your mum wouldn't be happy if I just let you wander around unsupervised, and neither would your grannies, Edie, or your parents, Hanna." She took a deep breath. "The world is an enormous place and Good Sister June could be anywhere. And look—maybe she doesn't even want to be found. She disappeared in the middle of the night and told us not to follow her. We need to respect that."

"Yes," said Hanna. "You're right."

There was a sudden and very loud pause before Good Sister Christine said, in quite a different tone of voice, "Am I? Are you—sure?"

"Yes," said Hanna again. "I got it wrong before. You're right. Not me."

"Oh," said Good Sister Christine. "Well, maybe I am. Okay. Yes." She looked deeply concerned. "Blimey."

Edie made a very French sound of disgust. "Hanna, are you—perhaps—possessed? Just a little bit?"

"Not at all," said Hanna, who was, in fact, having an idea.

"Are you having an idea?" said Calla in a very quiet and Picking Up On The Subtext sort of fashion.

"Yes," said Hanna in a very quiet and I Knew I Liked You sort of fashion. And then, louder, she said, "I really do think that we are here to go to school and we should do that, just as Good Sister Christine says, and wait for Good Sister June to come back when she's ready."

"Gosh, what an excellent idea," said Calla in her brightest and most unproblematic tones. "Good Sister Christine, you really mustn't worry about us. If one of us says that you don't have to worry about us then you don't. That's how it works. We are best friends and what one of us says, we all agree with."

When she finished speaking, Calla turned towards Edie and made a Look, It Would Really Help Us Out If You Joined In Right Now face.

Edie made an Actually I Am *Fully* Aware of What's Going On But It's Not Convincing If We All Agree

110

With Her At Once, Is It Now? face before turning back to Good Sister Christine. "As the dear Hanna and Calla have already said, there is nothing for you to worry about. We understand what you are saying and you must not worry about us. We are going to sleep in our beds and be such peaceful and quiet and good girls."[1]

"You will?"

The girls nodded.

Good Sister Christine looked at them with a sudden and sharp sense of relief. "I'm so sorry I had to say that to you—I mean, you don't know how happy that makes me. I can't worry about you three as well as Good Sister June. Thank you. I was so convinced you'd run off on one of your adventures but you've made the right choice. I knew I could trust you."

"Oh yes," said Hanna. "Always."

The moment that Good Sister Christine left the room, Hanna turned around to where Edie and Calla were standing. "Come with me," she said, "there's something I need to show you. Right now."

---

1 Which is such a remarkable statement for Edie Berger to make that Good Sister Christine should have picked up on it right there and then. But she did not, and I am glad because without it, there would be no Spun Sugar Cottage and I will tell you all about that remarkable place soon, I promise.

WHERE THE STORIES BEGIN

A library at any point in the day is special but a library on the first night of a new term is even more special. The library at the School of the Good Sisters was no exception to this rule. The sun was setting outside and the room was full of a thick, golden light. Several first years had begun to make an elaborate book fort in one corner of the room while the others were helping Sethi and Sabia Gopal set up a shadow puppet theatre in the other. In the middle of all of this, Ellen Beaufort and Eloise Taylor were making toasted ham and cheese sandwiches while Lucy Millais and Maisie Holloway were helping them out by eating all of the leftovers.

When Hanna opened the door on this night, every single girl in that room looked up and said hello to her. She smiled and waved back at them all before heading straight over to the still-messy desk that she'd discovered earlier that day. It was so strange, she thought, it had only been a few hours ago and yet it felt like it had been years.

Calla looked at the mess and then at Hanna and said, "What are you showing us, Han?"

Hanna gestured at the notebook. "I've never seen this

notebook before today and I know everything that's in this library. I've *read* everything in this library."

"And you have read them all at least twice," said Edie with some pride. "Go on."

"Well, I didn't realize it until I saw the note that Good Sister Christine showed us but then I worked it all out. This is in the same handwriting. This is Good Sister June's notebook. And isn't it strange that she was looking through it just before she left?"

"Indeed, my dear Hanna *pain au chocolat*, this is definitely A Clue," said Edie. "But what of the newspapers? Because if Good Sister June was here, then she was not just reading the notebook. All of these papers are here for a reason and we must find the meaning of that."

And so the three of them settled down to work. Edie began to sort through the newspapers while Calla and Hanna focused on the notebook itself. Hanna had flicked through it previously but it was only now that she began to realize just how magical a book it really was. Several pages were painted with pictures of cake and others had fragments of material glued in next to little notes that said: *curtains* or *chair cushions*. The colours of all of these had faded over the years but somehow only made the drawings and the material feel richer. Other pages still had handwritten notes about what fresh flowers could be put on the tables and which seasons they would be in bloom: *daffodils in spring and roses in winter and even petals on the cupcakes if we can.* And if all that were not enough, somebody had even written down a list of potential locations for the café. The names of the villages felt like spells as Hanna read them out: *"Filey. Cayton. Rutherford Bay. Whitby. Merlin Cove.* They're all local villages on the coast."

"Well if they're local, then we'd already know if this café existed so it doesn't," said Calla hungrily as she looked at one page. "And I don't understand why. It's perfect. I'd live here if I could."

Hanna nodded. "There's something else not making sense to me though. If this is Good Sister June's notebook, then why did she ever become a nun? And a teacher? Why isn't she living her best life in this café surrounded by the best cake?" She gestured at a page full of ingredients for a chocolate sponge. "Something doesn't add up."

"It's like my mum's coded book," said Calla, referencing an adventure that had taken place during her first term at the School of the Good Sisters. "It's a clue but you don't know how to completely understand it. Did she ever talk about anything like this to you?"

"No. If I ever asked her anything about her life outside of the school, she would just change the subject. I even thought for a while that she didn't exist before it. That she was, like, born a nun and was always an adult." And then, all of a sudden she saw it on one of the pages that Calla was turning over. "Hang on," she said, "Go back. There. Look. We've got proof of one thing at least." She took the notebook from Calla and held it out so that they could all read it.

We promise to be best friends for life.
We promise to run the best book-café ever.
And also, we promise to never, ever, make anything
   involving kale.

Signed by:

Lily Bishop,
Georgia Bishop
June Mortimer
June 7ᵗʰ 1955

Hanna pointed at the name *June Mortimer*. "That's got to be Good Sister June before she became a nun."

Calla did some rapid mental arithmetic. "The year would be right as well," she said, "Good Sister June is in her eighties now so that would make her fifteen or sixteen in 1955. Maybe this was her plan for what she was going to do after school and who she was going to do it with. A bakery bookshop café with her best friends. It sounds perfect."

Hanna nodded. "Yes," she said. "So what went wrong?"

THE LAST WORD

Hanna could not understand why or even how Good Sister June had kept all of this secret from her. The two of them had shared so much with each other in their long, lovely evenings in the library. Good Sister June knew everything about Hanna. She knew about how Hanna never knew what to say to her parents, and about how the school felt like the home that she had never really had, and about how the thought of leaving it all one day made her heart drop like a stone into water. She knew all of Hanna's secrets and here she was, keeping her own.

And then Hanna was distracted from thinking anything else because she had noticed something quite unusual about Edie Berger. Her friend had picked up one of the newspapers from the desk and begun to read it. This was not the unusual thing in itself. What was unusual were the sounds of disgust that made Edie sound very much like an angry train pulling into a station.

"Edie, are you okay?"

Edie looked up. "No I am not," she said. "There is a man trying to do nefarious things and oh, I cannot read any more because I will *explode*."

Hanna leant over and took the newspaper off her. "Then I'll read it for you. Make sure you don't explode until I'm done." She began to read the article aloud, and because I am a helpful author I shall write it all out below.

Exciting news for Little Hampden! Have you ever walked past the bakery just off the main street? It's been abandoned for years but it looks like it's going to be open again soon—but this time as the headquarters of Kale Paste, a business which sells food made out of, wait for it, a specially designed and patented kale paste formula.

We spoke to the soon-to-be owner, William George Bishop, for more information. "The rumours are true," he said, "Kale Paste makes healthy and nutritious food entirely out of kale paste. We have kale cakes and kale pastries and kale sausages and they're all so delicious that you'd never know that they were made out of nothing but kale. Why, you could eat nothing but Kale Paste for the rest of your life and be totally happy!

"We've been looking for headquarters for our business for a while and Little Hampden is perfect for it. We're also after some suitable premises nearby to turn into a factory (I've got my eyes on the perfect building already!) so we can make Kale Paste on an industrial scale and turn this village into a kale paradise!

"We really do have big dreams for Kale Paste," Bishop informed the Hampden Herald. *"I spent my childhood eating nothing but vegetables like this and it's made me the man I am today. My vision is to see everybody in Little Hampden eating nothing but kale but that's a while ahead, of course. We're talking with the Mayor about how we can make that happen. It will be so good for the local children and so much easier for the nearby School of the Good Sisters if they adopt a Kale Paste diet. Why, we're already speaking with their governors—"*

It was at this point that Hanna put down the paper. She stared at the others. "Did I just read what I think I read? He's speaking to our governors?" The article was a week old. Who knew what might have happened since then.

"They'd never say yes," said Calla faintly.

"But what if they did? What would happen to our cakes and biscuits? Good Sister Honey's apple pies, baked potatoes, scrambled eggs on buttery toast...?"

"They would disappear," said Edie. "All of it would go and be replaced by this Kale Paste. I will not have it. I will not, I tell you. I will not have my school threatened like this! I will not!"

Hanna took a deep breath. She picked up the paper and continued to read.

"—but for now, we're starting with the bakery. It's been in the family for years but we never did anything useful with

it. But now, my Great-Aunt Lily has decided to let me take charge and bring the family business into the twenty-first century. Of course, this is only due to her failing health and while I'm so very sad for that, I'm also very excited for the opportunities that lie ahead."

Edie looked up. "Failing health? But what does this mean?"

"It means that she's dying," said Hanna. It was an expression she'd come across in one of the old books that she'd read and she had never forgotten it. It had seemed such a delicate way to express something so sad.

Calla nodded. Her father had died when she was very young and although she had never known him, the thought of anybody being excited over his death made her feel a little bit sick inside. "It's awful," she said slowly. "How can anybody even think that way about someone?"

"It's horrible," said Hanna. "It's just horrible. All of it."

"And all of it will be stopped," said Edie. She squeezed Hanna's arm gently. "I know that we must solve the mystery of Good Sister June, but first, you must give me a moment to address this. We must have somewhere to bring her back to and that somewhere must not—*shall not*—serve Kale Paste." And with that, she climbed on top of the desk and then, in a voice that would have been heard in the middle of a force nine gale, said, "My beautiful friends, a moment of your time if you please!"

And all of a sudden, every single girl in the room turned to look at her.

As indeed, they always would.

THE FIGHTING
WORDS OF
EDIE BERGER

"**W**e have been back at school but a day and yet darkness already threatens us! Not only has our Good Sister June disappeared for reasons we do not yet know but this man—here, Calla, show them his photograph, no Eloise, she is showing you the picture of the man and not of the house that is for sale—look at him! Does he not look precisely like a slice of ham and not even the nice sort of ham? Well—he is trying to ban cakes and biscuits and all things delicious from our school and replace them with a paste made entirely out of kale! Imagine it, my little *tartiflettes*, everything in this school that you eat will be made from kale! Kale Paste, everywhere you look! Can you imagine it?"

At this point, several of the more impressionable first years imagined so hard that they promptly fainted, whilst behind them, the rest were already building anti-kale barricades in front of the recipe books.

Edie noted all of this with some satisfaction before she continued. "Would you like to know the worst part of it all? It is that a bakery, a building that should be dedicated to joy, will make nothing but monstrosities instead. Kale-filled cakes and pastries! Kale biscuits with a sandwich of kale cream! So! He must be stopped and he will. From tomorrow, we shall protest! Prepare yourselves, my little pâtisseries! Sleep the sleep of the noble and the righteous this night, for tomorrow we fight!"

And at *this* point, the first years who hadn't fainted started to chatter excitedly about potential protest slogans[1] while several of the older girls, who had been previously involved in Edie's battles against the dark and unjust, came over to the desk. They were led by Rose Bastable who, helpfully enough, had brought sandwiches. She handed them round to the small group of girls and said, "Does this kale business happen to have something to do with Good Sister June not being around for the welcome back tea?"

"Or all day," said Jia Liu as she bit into her sandwich.

"Whatever Good Sister Christine might want us to believe," said Ellen Beaufort darkly.

Hanna nodded. "She's not on holiday. She's gone. Somewhere. We don't know. She left a note that told Good Sister Christine that she was in charge now and not to worry."

"Which means that there is something to worry about," said Rose.

---

[1] MAKE CAKE NOT WAR, YOUR COUNTRY NEEDS BISCUITS and FORGET VEG, HAVE A NICE SPONGE INSTEAD. (They were planning a particularly big placard for this last one.)

"Precisely," said Edie. "Something is ROTTEN in the state of Denmark."[1]

"We're not in Denmark," said Rose.

"I am *aware* of that," said Edie.

"The only problem is that we're not quite sure where Good Sister June has gone and we need to work it out," said Calla in a Maybe We Should Focus On The Important Stuff Right Now tone of voice. She gestured at the desk behind her and realized, for the first time, that Hanna had gone back to look through the rest of the newspapers. Very quietly, she finished her sandwich and moved over to her friend. "Hanna," she said, "are you all right? Edie's just done one of her deeply inspiring speeches and I don't know if you're quite as deeply inspired as you should be. I mean, I can cover for you for a while but she's going to notice soon and offer you a course of remedial lectures when she does."

Hanna gave her the quick sort of smile you can only give a best friend who understands you completely. "I'm all right," she said. "I was thinking about all of the things that are happening—the newspapers and the book and Good Sister June's note and her disappearance—and then it hit me. Bishop. The kale man's name is Bishop. So are the people in the notebook. He's taking over a bakery that's been in the family forever. The people in the notebook are obsessed with bakeries. And if Good Sister June was reading all about this kale man—"

1 This is a quote from a play called *Hamlet* by William Shakespeare.

"And his terminally ill great-aunt who owns a bakery—"

The two of them stared at each other.

"Well," said Edie, as she came over to join them.[1] "Have you worked it all out then?"

---

1 Carrying, might I add, a further sandwich in each hand.

IN WHICH WE LEARN A
LOT ABOUT KALE PASTE

Every newspaper on that desk was from the last week and they all mentioned William Bishop and his plans for Kale Paste and Little Hampden. And now that they had worked out the connections between him and the notebook, Hanna saw connections on every single page. The sketches of the bakery shelves in the notebook were the same as the ones in the background of William's photo. The font on the sign that had been copied into the book was exactly the same font as William's proposed sign for *The Kale Paste Emporium (Ask Us How Much We Love Kale!)*.

She reached for the nearest newspaper, and began to read it out loud.

"Kale Paste can be shaped into any food that you want and, providing you treat it right during the manufacturing process, it can taste of anything you want it to—with undertones of kale, of course! And who doesn't love a hint of kale in everything they eat?"

At the bottom of the article was a quote from the Mayor.

> *"It's going to be so great for the village," said*
> *Mayor Dominic Burton of Little Hampden.*
> *"William is a man full of vision. He's very*
> *exciting to work with—he's so generous and*
> *giving—and Kale Paste really is delicious. He*
> *had me convinced when he served me fish and*
> *chips made entirely out of kale! Yum!"*

"That's the most ridiculous thing anybody has ever said," said Calla, who was reading this over Hanna's shoulder.

Hanna nodded and picked up another newspaper. This one had a picture of William on the front of it:

> *"I've been trying to take over the premises for a*
> *while now but my relatives took a lot of persuad-*
> *ing," Mr Bishop tells the* Post. *"It's understand-*
> *able, really. They've owned the building since the*
> *fifties. But what worked then doesn't work now.*
> *There's no space for a bakery in my vision. Little*
> *Hampden needs Kale Paste. Our children need*
> *Kale Paste. We need to make the right decision*
> *for them."*

Halfway down the page was a picture of William with the Mayor. Hanna stared at it with some fascination. She could not quite understand how both men could look quite so much like ham sandwiches. They were so very... pink.

And our new Mayor agrees! "I'm totally invested
in William's ideas and so we've been working on
some special new laws for the local businesses.
We want Kale Paste to thrive here and become
the next big thing. That means helping him to
find premises to turn into a factory and also
supporting him in getting it to everybody who
lives in Little Hampden. Our children. Our
adults. Everybody in between. We'll all be eating
Kale Paste!"

"This sounds horrific," said Rose Bastable darkly. "How do we stop him? And how quickly can we do it? And why does he look a little bit like a ham sandwich?"

"I would like to propose a *tiny* poisoning," said Edie.

Maisie Holloway tactfully ignored this as she sat down at the table with them. She gestured at one of the articles. "Nobody normal loves kale that much."

"Nobody *anybody* loves kale that much," said Lucy Millais, who had been showing the first years how to make water bombs.[1] She pushed herself onto the other half of Maisie's chair. "And while I'm all in favour of protesting the socks off him because I don't think my dad would forgive me if I didn't,[2] is the protest actually going to bring Good Sister June back? She

[1] Carefully.

[2] Lucy's father runs a very successful bakery called *All You Knead Is Love* and if you are ever passing, then I recommend the salted caramel shortbread because it is very near to perfection.

won't know anything about the protest if she's not here to see it."

A long silence followed this.

"What did her note say again?" said Jia Liu softly.

"That she didn't want anybody to follow her," replied Calla.

Hanna leant forward on her elbows. She felt a little lightheaded. It was as if all of them were coming to a life-changing moment and she was the only one who had realized it. "Technically, the note was addressed to Good Sister Christine and she was telling *her* not to follow her. And Good Sister Christine hasn't gone anywhere but to bed."[1]

Edie gave her a swift look of pride. "I knew my lectures on beating the legal system would be useful for you! And, my friends, Hanna is right. This is technically a loophole and one that we can exploit."

"You'll have to exploit it without Good Sister Christine knowing anything then," said Maisie. "She's being very adult right now and it's not a good look."

"She's worried about Good Sister June," said Calla, who had spent much of her life before school around adults and so often understood them more than the other girls did. "Adults sometimes try to do the right thing when they're not sure what the right thing is and so are really very talented at doing the absolutely wrong thing instead."

1 This was not quite true as you (and indeed Hanna) will shortly find out.

And that is the sort of sentence that might not make sense when you look at it but makes perfect sense when you think it through.

"That makes perfect sense when you think it through," said Sethi Gopal. "It's not easy for any of us. It's not right without Good Sister June being here. It would be like me having to be somewhere without Sabia."

Sabia shuddered. "Don't even say it."

Sethi and Sabia did not often speak about their twinship like this and so, when they did, the girls all paid attention. Even the first years paused in their revolutionary song compositions[1] to listen, and then, when they had finished, they doubled the intensity of their efforts. They would protest against Kale Paste because even the thought of it was horrific but also, in some way, it would distract everybody from being so sad and might possibly bring Good Sister June home to them.[2]

"I think I know how to find her," said Hanna quietly. She gestured at the notebook. "There's a list of seaside towns in here and all we have to do is go to them and look for somebody who knows Great-Aunt Lily Bishop who used to run a bakery in Little Hampden. It's more clues than we've had for some of our other adventures."

"And we have a motive for her suddenly leaving," said Calla. She squeezed Hanna's arm in a supportive If You

[1] "KALE KALE ALWAYS STALE, WE HOPE THE NASTY KALE MAN FAILS."

[2] And I can tell you that when Good Sister June heard about this, she had a Tiny Cry of her very own.

128

Need A Tiny Cry Then Now's The Moment To Have One sort of fashion. "If she read all of this stuff and realized that somebody was trying to get rid of all of the cakes in school and replace them with Kale Paste and that her beloved best friend's bakery is at the heart of it, and that her beloved best friend is actually *dying*, then that's enough to upset anybody."

Hanna squeezed Calla's arm back in a Yes, I'd Appreciate A Tiny Cry At Some Point But I Will Do It Once We Find Good Sister June And Not Before fashion. "We—Calla and Edie and I—will go and find Good Sister June and tell her that she's going to be okay because when you're very sad and feeling all alone, that's when you need telling that sort of thing the most. And we'll bring her back to the school. We'll bring her home."

A SMALL TIN OF ANCHOVIES

Rose Bastable bounced to her feet. "Well, we'll make sure that you've got something to bring her back to. That man will not be able to do anything without us watching. We'll set up shifts and keep an eye on him round the clock. Calla, we'll send you updates on your phone and let you know how it's going."

"A part of me wants to stay and fight alongside you," said Edie dreamily. "But I cannot. It is not my destiny." She turned to the nearest first years who were rapidly stifling their tears at this news. "My tiny numerous chums! I must go with Calla and Hanna for they are about to embark upon a noble quest full of death and peril and my place is at their side under such circumstances. But! You must provide me with updates of your fight against evil while I am gone!"

One first year wiped her eyes. "We'll send you letters every day."

"We'll email."

"We'll send pigeons."

"We'll join in the Twilight Barking."

"Or," said Hanna, "you could phone Calla and leave a message."

"Yes! And if the phones become compromised,[1] then we shall turn to radio!" said Edie brightly. "Ellen! You are practically minded! I have installed a radio receiver on the North Tower and so, if you run a wire from there to your bedroom (perhaps a little light welding may be needed!) you will be able to send and receive anything. My call sign is *Macaron*. Yours, I think, will be *Pasta Salad*. So! We shall leave tonight!"

Calla shook her head. "We'll leave tomorrow morning. There are no trains or buses or anything this late at night. If Good Sister June did leave early in the morning then she would have got the train to Filey. It's the first one from the station that goes anywhere."

"What about a taxi?" said Sethi Gopal. She leant forward and rested her elbows on the table. "Good Sister June might have got one of those. She might not have gone near the station at all."

"Her favourite book is *The Railway Children*," said Hanna. "She once spent hours telling me about it. There's no way she wouldn't have got on a train."

"So it's the station then. That means you can cut through the woods to get there quicker."

Calla nodded. "We can get the morning train to Filey. I'll check the times before I go to bed but I think it's about seven-thirty. That gives us time to pack our bags, get some sleep and then go first thing."

---

1 This is a fancy way of saying "just in case somebody who we don't want to listen is, in fact, listening".

Edie looked thoughtful. "For me, I think I shall include a small tub of olives, a tin of anchovies and perhaps also some *pâté de campagne* and light *charcuterie* for my elevenses. Elevenses! A beautiful invention! By one of my ancestors, did I ever tell you this?"

Rose Bastable raised her eyebrows. "You can *charcuterie* and elevenses all you want but you'll never get out of school without being discovered. You *know* everybody gets up early here. Good Sister Gwendolyn does her morning yoga class and Good Sister Honey goes out foraging in the wood. Everybody's going to see you and stop you before you get anywhere. You need a distraction."

"Well," said Hanna, who had actually been having an idea about that. "I've actually been having an idea about that."

WELDING AT MIDNIGHT

Once Hanna had outlined the details of the distraction, the girls parted and headed off to their respective bedrooms to sleep or, in the case of Ellen Beaufort and Eloise Taylor, to do some rapid welding on the roof outside their Tower window. Once this was completed, Ellen and Eloise finally went to sleep with the blissful knowledge that their part in the distraction was done and that they were getting breakfast in bed as a thank you.

The only people who did not sleep or weld were the members of the North Tower bedroom. This was because they were packing their bags full of important things for the adventure which lay ahead. These things were flannels,[1] biscuits, spare socks, six freshly baked cheese scones that had just been borrowed from the kitchens, one hairbrush to share between the three of them, an entire Victoria sponge cake, a tub of chocolate spread and a spare pair of shoes each. To this Calla added a train timetable and a phone charger; Edie added a spatula, a compass and

---

1 If I am honest, they were not completely sure what a flannel was or what it was used for but they knew that Good Sister Christine loved them and so that was good enough.

a roll full of wire; and Hanna added a copy of *Eustacia Goes to the Chalet School* just in case she needed to do an emergency story time.

When they were finished, Edie took the bags and piled them up next to the door of their bedroom. "So! We can now pick these up the moment we awaken tomorrow. But! Calla! My dear little *beignet*! That timetable of yours is enormous. It will make your bag weigh twice as much as it should. Are you sure we cannot simply trust to our instincts as adventurers and follow our hearts towards the horizon?"

"It's the perfect thing for an adventure," said Calla in a deeply practical fashion. "It's basically the internet but for trains. If we're going to be somewhere and my phone doesn't have enough signal or battery, then we'll need this. Otherwise we'll never know when the trains leave and we'll be stuck there forever."

Even Edie was convinced by this argument.

"Even I am convinced by this argument," said Edie. "But do you know what I am also convinced by? Going to bed. Tomorrow, we adventure. But tonight, we sleep."

And so they did.

BY THE PRICKING OF MY THUMBS, SOMETHING DISTRACTING THIS WAY COMES

Even Good Sister Christine slept well that night and that was something that she had not expected. The moment that she had finished speaking to Hanna, Calla and Edie, she had gone off to Good Sister June's bedroom and sat on the edge of her friend's bed for a very long time. If you had asked her what she was thinking about, I do not think that she would have been able to tell you. All she knew was that she had suddenly started to feel very old and tired and she did not know how to deal with it at all.

When she eventually left Good Sister June's bedroom and headed slowly towards her own, she passed Good Sister Paulette in the corridor. The older nun had her hands wrapped around an enormous mug of hot chocolate, which was topped with marshmallows and whipped cream. And when she saw the look that Good Sister Christine gave this, Good Sister Paulette promptly offered it to her.

"Take it," she said. "You need this more than me."

"I can't," said Good Sister Christine.

"You can," said Good Sister Paulette. "And you should and you will. You've had a lot to deal with today. All of us have found it hard with June's absence but you, I think, with all of your new responsibilities, will have found it the hardest."

And the soft wisdom of this made Good Sister Christine have a Tiny Cry right there and then in the corridor.[1]

Good Sister Paulette's response was swift and the same that she would have given to any member of the school. She took Good Sister Christine to her bedroom and when she had put on her pyjamas and finished the hot chocolate, Good Sister Paulette tucked her into her bed and gave her a quick hug and when she woke up the next day, Good Sister Christine felt, at last, as if she might be able to be the Headmistress after all.

She said, "Good morning," to Good Sister Honey as they passed each other in the corridor and Good Sister Honey pressed a tray full of freshly baked chocolate croissants into her arms. She handed these over to Good Sister Gwendolyn and the film club who were setting up for a morning viewing of *Million Dollar Mermaid*[2] before then dodging the early morning camouflage class and Sally Campbell and Jia Liu's very convincing rendition of a grandfather clock.

---

1 A Tiny Cry is the sort of cry that you do when you are a Little Bit Overwhelmed by everything that is going on and just want a moment to catch your breath and figure out your thoughts.

2 I asked Good Sister Gwendolyn to sum this film up in three words and here they are: "Dancing. In the Water. Amazing." Technically that is five words but she distracted me with a pink wafer so she got away with it.

"Oh how did you know it was us?" said Sally as she disentangled herself from Jia's shoulders.

"Elbows," said Good Sister Christine. "Always a give-away. Have a custard cream and then try again."

As she walked through the building, she realized that even though Good Sister June was not here to see it, the school was getting along with its life. Admittedly there was an enormous group of first years on the lawn outside making protest placards and another enormous group of first years practising songs that seemed to be entirely about kale for some reason[1] but these were not unusual things to happen at the School of the Good Sisters and so Good Sister Christine did not let herself be bothered by it. Instead she made her way through the girls' bedrooms and woke up anybody who was still asleep—"It's a wonderful day, Eloise, get out there and enjoy it. Take a biscuit."—before heading into the Hall to get her own breakfast.[2]

Alas, it was just as she was picking up her knife and fork to tuck in that Hanna's distraction began.

And a tiny[3] explosion[4] went off in the fifth-floor laboratory.

1 "Two! Four! Six! Eight! Kale-based food is not that great!"
2 Scrambled eggs on buttery toast with two small and perfectly crisp sausages on the side.
3 Yet incredibly well-controlled and in fact, completely safe.
4 You must promise me NEVER to explode anything unless you have been to Good Sister Paulette's How To Explode Things Safely class beforehand.

FINDING ELIZA ZACEK

There are many things that you might do under such circumstances but the nuns of the School of the Good Sisters chose the wisest. This was to stop whatever they were doing, grab the nearest pack of emergency biscuits,[1] and then begin to clear the rooms and corridors of girls. The older girls grabbed anybody who was looking lost or panicked and took them outside and towards the trees where the school was meant to gather in such moments of crisis. It was a complete coincidence that every girl who had been in the library last night was already there to greet them.[2]

Meanwhile, Hanna and Calla and Edie picked up their rucksacks and climbed out of the North Tower bedroom window and onto the roof.

And while all of *that* was happening, Good Sister Christine picked up a rucksack of her very own which was full of all of the important things that a Headmistress needs with her when her school might be a little bit on

1 There is at least one in every first aid box.
2 This included a very snoozy Ellen Beaufort and Eloise Taylor who were having a Tiny Nap on the shoulder of Sethi and Sabia Gopal respectively.

fire. Along with practical things like the school register, an emergency flannel and a hard-boiled egg, it contained things like Good Sister June's favourite pen, a photograph of Good Sister Gladys,[1] and several unopened packs of custard creams. Good Sister Christine slung the rucksack over her shoulder and did a final check of the school before heading out to join everybody and take the register.

And just as she read out "Sally Campbell", Hanna and Calla and Edie reached the object that Ellen Beaufort and Eloise Taylor had left for them: a newly welded together ladder. Hanna was the first to climb down and when she was sure that the coast was clear, she motioned for the others to follow her. They paused only to hide the ladder in a particularly dark and secret patch of ivy before making their way into the woods.

And by the time Good Sister Christine had reached "Eliza Zacek" on her register, the three girls from the North Tower bedroom were long gone but had also answered their names on the register and so had not officially gone anywhere at all.

Ah yes.

Let me explain.

---

1 The school's first Headmistress.

HOW TO BE HERE
BUT ALSO THERE

When Good Sister Christine had reached Calla's
name on the register, she had looked up and expected to
see Calla's bright yellow hair in front of her. Instead of
this, she was greeted by a girl wearing a very haphazardly
dyed wig[1] who said, "I'm here!" before disappearing back
into the crowd. This was clearly a Suspicious Moment
but there was a lot on Good Sister Christine's mind and
so she decided to let it slide. She did not, however, let it
slide very far because when she reached Hanna's name
on the register, something else happened. Rather than
hearing Hanna's voice, she had heard somebody who did
not sound remotely like her say, "I'm here," in a rather
panicked fashion before panicking just a little bit more
and adding, "Also I *really* like books!"[2]

It was at this point that Good Sister Christine began
to connect the dots and realize that Something Unusual

[1] The girl was Maisie Holloway and the wig had been dyed late the
night before with custard powder. I do not want to think about what
might have happened if it had started raining.
[2] This was Sethi Gopal, who is fabulous at many things but not great
under pressure, it has to be said.

was happening. And because the things that happened to Hanna and Calla tended to involve the third member of the North Tower bedroom, she glanced over to where Edie was standing. She had answered her name in a very convincing fashion when Good Sister June had called it. The only problem was that the girl[1] who had responded was currently standing in a Very Still And Trying Not To Draw Attention to Herself sort of manner which was, under the circumstances, now doing the complete opposite.

Good Sister Christine took a deep breath. She waited until the girls and the nuns in front of her were distracted before she slipped around to the front of the school. She checked again to make sure that she hadn't been followed before heading down to the school kitchens. As she had suspected, there was an individual in there who hadn't noticed any of the morning's events.

"Hello," said Good Sister Christine to this person.[2] "We had a small explosion and a lot of smoke go off but it's all all right now. Were you here all along?"

"No," said the person. They looked deeply confused. "I was picking mushrooms for the morning omelettes and then when I got back nobody was here so I got *very* confused."

Good Sister Christine decided to focus on the important stuff. "Did you see anybody while you were out? I'm missing three girls from the register."

1 Sabia Gopal who, as an experienced method actor, had eaten fifteen *crêpes au chocolat* to get into the role.
2 I shall tell you who this is in a few chapters but for now it must be a little bit mysterious.

"Would one of them happen to have hair the colour of a Battenberg?"

"Yes!" said Good Sister Christine. She felt a sudden and almost overwhelming sense of relief. "Was she with two other girls? One of them would be small and fierce, and the other girl has red hair and would probably be carrying a book."

"Yes," said the person.

"Yes to the hair colour? The description? Which part?"

"All of it. I saw them. All three of them. I'm sure about it."

A rush of relief almost overwhelmed Good Sister Christine. "The girls—what were they doing?"

The moment that she finished speaking, she realized that she already knew.

"They were walking through the woods. They all had rucksacks on. I thought they were out foraging but then they walked right past the best patch—"

"They're going to find her," said Good Sister Christine. She felt a sudden and almost infinite sense of happiness rise up inside her. "They've gone to find Good Sister June and I am going to let it happen. It's not the adult thing to do or the thing that a normal Headmistress would do but I'm neither and I never will be and I thought that I had to be but I don't. I don't." She grinned at the person standing in front of her. "Okay. Listen to me—right now— there's a job that I need you to do. I can't leave the school so you're going to have to be there for those girls when I can't. I want you to follow the girls and keep them safe.

Do anything that you need to do to make that happen but don't let yourself be seen. They don't need to know that I know what's happening."

"I'm not sure if I know what's happening," said the person with some confusion. "Is the start of term always like this?"

"Yes," said Good Sister Christine. "Listen—I want you to keep those girls you saw safe. Keep them out of trouble. Make something up if they realize you're following them. But for now, just keep them safe and help them find Good Sister June and bring her home. Does that all make sense? Can you do that for me—for them?"

The person looked at her and nodded. "Of course."

And so the quest for Good Sister June gained another member.

ON THE WAY TO AN ADVENTURE

"I've been thinking about what went wrong between Good Sister June and her friends," said Hanna as she walked steadily through the woods with Calla and Edie at her side.[1] "They were *best friends forever*. Perhaps they drifted apart. But I think it must have been something big to make them abandon all their café plans. Like, the worst sort of dramatic."

Edie nodded. "Like an English person trying to make a *croque madame*. The secret is to select the right kind of cheese and alas, they never do." All of a sudden, she crouched down and tied a loop of string around a tree. She pulled it tight before knotting it around a tree at the other side of the path.

"What is the right sort of cheese?" said Hanna.

"And also what are you doing?" said Calla.

"Gruyere," said Edie. "And I shall explain all shortly."

Hanna decided to let it go. She had been friends with Edie long enough to know that she would tell all when

[1] And an extra person following them, but you will learn more about them shortly.

144

she was ready. "Well, whatever it was and whatever you're doing, can you imagine just letting your friends go like that?"

"Adults are remarkably strange individuals," said Edie. "By the way, can one of you hold this for a moment? Thank you." She gave Calla a stale and very hard cheese scone before reaching into her own pocket and producing a ball of string. She knotted a neat loop of this together before throwing it over one of the branches high above her. "The scone, if you please."

Calla passed over the scone.[1]

Edie knotted the string around it before then twisting the entire affair around one of the lower branches. She gave the string a tug and the cheese scone fell directly towards her head. Or, at least, to where her head would have been if she had been an adult. "Perfection," she said, placing the cheese scone back onto the branch.

"I know that Calla's already asked this, but what are you doing?"

"I am preparing," said Edie. She suddenly pulled a spatula out of her bag and balanced it carefully on a stone. She weighted one end down with a ball of mud while the other, she left sticking up in the air.

"Don't step on this," she warned the others. "Let us discuss, instead, how we get through that."

That was the slope that lay before them, thick with bramble and tall, wild clumps of grass entwined with

1 Which is a sentence I thought I'd never write.

bindweed and raw, sharp-edged thorns. It was clear that nobody had been this way for years. Everywhere that Hanna looked, she saw an impossible path. And yet giving up and going to the station on the roads instead was equally impossible.

Hanna took a deep breath. "It's not even seven-fifteen," she said. "I'm not giving up before we've even begun. We have to get to the station by half-past if we're to catch the train. We don't have time to go by the road."

"Courage!" said Edie. "We shall do this together! That is how we *always* win. Calla, you come and walk behind me, and, Hanna, you go behind Calla. I will find us a path and as long as you follow, then you will be fine. Tread precisely in my footsteps. Watch out for branches that may spring back as I push past. And remember that every step forward is one more towards victory, my dear apple strudels! Let our bloody colours wave! And either victory or else a grave!"[1]

Calla looked at Hanna.

Hanna looked at Calla.

"Can we have victory?" said Calla with a sudden grin. "I like victory best."

Hanna nodded. "Yes," she said. "We'll have victory."

And slowly but surely the three of them started to climb up the slope towards the station.

---

1 This is a quote from a play by William Shakespeare. The play is *Henry VI, Part 3* and I am not surprised that Edie remembered it word for word because it is absolutely full of Inspiring Fighting Bits.

A HARD CHEESE SCONE

The three girls made slow progress up the hill. Their feet kept getting caught in the weeds and then when they did get them free, they'd stand on a piece of mud or some wet and slick patch of undergrowth and find themselves sliding back into each other.

"Are we anywhere near the top yet?" said Calla as she ducked under a low branch, slipped on some mud and somehow managed to dodge a bunch of angry looking nettles all at once.

Hanna nodded. "That's the station car park over there." She had spotted the curve of shiny cars in between all of the overgrown shrubbery that surrounded them. "We just need to get over the fence."

"And if we do it quickly, we'll be able to catch the seven-thirty to Filey," said Calla approvingly.

"And also escape the person who is following us," said Edie.

Hanna stared at her remarkable friend. "By what? By who? When did you know?"

Edie looked deeply smug. "Not only did I hear how the twigs broke under the heavy tread of their boot, and their so very loud breathing when they followed us across a particularly difficult bit, but I also heard them say 'ow' when they were clonked on the head by a stale cheese scone and then I heard them say 'ow' again as they fell over a perfectly placed trip wire. Oh, I am really very deeply skilled in tradecraft! But! Enough of my remarkable talents! Find me a tree close to this fence, my forever friends, and make it a good one."

Without another word being said, the three girls split along the edge of the fence. Edie went left while Hanna and Calla went right. They were almost at the edge of the car park and wondering if they would ever find a suitable tree before all of a sudden, they did. It had grown through the fence so that part of it was on one side and part of it on the other, and the branches did not bend or break however much weight they put on them.[1]

Calla put her fingers to her lips and let out an ear-piercing whistle.

Edie was at their sides within seconds.

Hanna gestured at the tree. "Is this good enough?"

Edie nodded. She shimmied to the top of it before then, very carefully, making her way over to the other side of the fence. She nodded again with satisfaction before climbing back to where Hanna and Calla were standing. "Pass me the bags," she said. "And then—Calla—you come up next after me, and then Hanna after you. I can help

[1] I must emphasize at this point that you are not to even think of climbing a tree like this unless you have been to Good Sister Paulette's Tree Climbing Masterclass and even then, you are not to think about climbing a tree until she is with you to help you out.

you up if you need it and Hanna will be there to catch you if you fall. Quickly though, before we are joined by our mysterious friend."

Calla gave her a grateful look. She had not been at the school as long as Hanna or Edie and so sometimes her abilities in climbing or camouflage or eating fifteen biscuits one after the other were not quite as advanced as the others.

"Oh, well done," said Edie, as she helped Calla make her way up the tree. "There. Stop. Test your footing first. Only proceed when you are completely sure of your footing and supervised by somebody as brilliant as me—there. Excellent. Now make sure that you keep your legs relaxed and then lower yourself down—perfect!"

Hanna was next to scramble up the tree. Edie helped her over the spiky edge of the fence as if she'd been doing it all her life before Calla watched her down the other side. Once Hanna had both feet on the floor, Edie dropped down lightly beside her. She patted Calla approvingly on the shoulder and said, "You have got so much better!" before turning back to look through the fence.

In the distance, there was a faint and rather pain-filled, "Ow."

"Aha," said Edie with some satisfaction. "Our follower has discovered the spatula."

HOW TO LOOK YOUR ENEMY
SQUARE IN THE FACE

I do not know if you have ever awaited the arrival of a mysterious enemy in a train station but just in case you haven't, here are my top tips. You must find somewhere that is far enough away to make sure that you're safe and out of danger and you must also have an emergency custard cream to hand to provide both an energy boost and also a welcome distraction.

Calla glanced up at the departures board as they walked past it. "The train's due in ten minutes. All we've got to do is not get caught before then."

They sat down on a bench, halfway down the platform, and looked over at the fence. They did not have long to wait. All of a sudden there was the sharp snap of branches underfoot and the outline of an enormous man appearing from the undergrowth. The only problem was that he was still just far enough away that they couldn't see who he was.

Hanna inhaled. She counted to ten. She exhaled. "How long until the train comes?"

"Nine minutes," said Calla. "By the way, have I ever told you about the time that my mum made me watch a film about dinosaurs, ages ago, just so she could point out all of the scientific mistakes that the writers had made?"[1]

"No," said Hanna, "you have not."

"Well, there was a bit in it where one of the dinosaurs—the tyrannosaurus rex—got out of its pen and it looked just like that man looks right now."

It was a very accurate description. The man's feet were so enormous and his legs so tall that rather than slipping and sliding down the hill like the girls had, he was managing to make it look as if it was not even there at all. As he reached the fence itself, he paused to catch his breath and a soft breeze rolled across the station, over the tracks, and all the way up to where the girls were sitting.

Instinctively Edie leant forward to sniff the air. An intrigued expression crossed her face. "There are *pains au chocolat* in that man's bag and I suspect that they have been freshly baked today. I am both intrigued and yet more suspicious! He plans to distract us with baked goods! We must not trust him! We must resist!"

"Hang on," said Hanna, who was rapidly realizing something very important about the man.

"That is the key to good fence climbing, yes," said Edie. "Hang on with all of your might and do not fall! He is failing at both! Good!"

---

[1] If you did not know, ducks are descended from dinosaurs. Here is a duck joke to celebrate the occasion: why do ducks fly south for the winter? Because it is too far to walk.

"No," said Hanna. "I think I know him. I think I even saw him in the school kitchen earlier."

"I think I know him too," said Calla, who was rapidly realizing something similar. She stared at Hanna. "Why is he even here? What's he doing?"

"I didn't think he'd come back after what happened."

"Do you think he's been at the school then?"

"How else would he have noticed us?"

"What are you two saying?" said Edie, who had not paid attention to any of this. "Look—if he comes closer, I will throw a circle of cave-aged Gruyere[1] at his head and then you must both run whilst I tackle him and take him down."

"Don't throw the cheese,"[2] said Hanna. "Edie—look at him. Properly. Now imagine him with foam on his head in the middle of the school and next to a slightly evil Headmistress who is about to get her comeuppance."

Edie's eyes suddenly brightened. "Yes! You are right! I do know this man!"

"Exactly," said Hanna. "Our follower is Gareth Angus MacDonald and now we have to figure out what we're going to do about that."

1 A very hard and very smelly cheese.
2 A valuable lesson for *all* of us.

A LITTLE BIT LIKE
COMING HOME

The man's name was indeed Gareth Angus MacDonald and if you have read one of my other books, then you, like the girls, will have already met him. If you have not, then I will tell you a little bit about him now otherwise what follows will make very little sense.[1] He is an enormous man with feet the size of hay bales and hands the size of cereal bowls. He had spent his entire life wanting to be a pâtisserie chef and it had never worked out for him. Not many people believed that somebody as big and as scary as Gareth had the skill to create tiny cakes of infinite beauty and so he had never been given a chance. Luckily enough that has all now changed and if you ever get the chance to go to his bakery—

Ah. Spoilers. I'll tell you all about *that* shortly.

Gareth's first trip to the School of the Good Sisters had been during Calla's first term. He had been hired to do Evil Things but had then decided to do Good Things instead. The first of those good things had been to surrender to the police and tell them about everything

---

1 Rather like a chocolate cake with raisins in it.

that had been happening. And the second had been to apologize to Good Sister June when she had come to see him in prison.

"I'm so sorry," he had told her. "I made bad choices."

"We all make bad choices," said Good Sister June. "What matters is what you do when people offer you good ones."

And then she had offered Gareth a job.

"When you come out of prison, I would like you to come and work at the school," she said. "Good Sister Honey needs help in the kitchens and you, I think, will be the right person to do that. I know that last time you were at the school it didn't go well. This time, I think it will be different. I think that *you* are different."

He had stared at her.

"I'm serious," she said. "You have a job with us. If you would like it, that is."

"I would like it very much," said Gareth. "I would like it very much indeed."[1]

And so, that August, on the day that he was released from prison, Gareth walked over the hills and straight to the door of the School of the Good Sisters. The pupils were still on holiday and so he devoted himself to looking after the nuns until they arrived. He made Good Sister Gwendolyn the layer cake from *Sleeping Beauty* and propped it up with a sweeping brush just like in the film,

[1] And so, just as Sarah Bishop had rescued June all those years ago, Good Sister June had rescued Gareth Angus MacDonald.

so that she could eat a slice while watching it on the big screen. For Good Sister Honey, he mastered sweet honey cakes that were barely as big as her thumb but exploded with delicious stickiness the moment that you bit into them, and for Good Sister Robin, who had spent her childhood at a boarding school in the Austrian Alps, he perfected a rich Sachertorte with a glaze so clear that she could see her own face in it. And after he discovered that Good Sister Paulette lived for the times when she could take to the skies and relive her fighter pilot days, he recreated the entire school out of gingerbread and included a tiny model of her helicopter as it came in to land.

Within days the nuns loved him and within weeks he was the happiest that he had ever been.

And he was the greatest gift that Good Sister Christine could have sent to Hanna, Calla and Edie.

THE ART OF ICING
ANYTHING

"**I** saw you leaving the school and I thought, well, they look like they need help," said Gareth, as he explained everything to the girls.[1] "I don't know what you're trying to do but it looks like an important something and that's the sort of something I want to help with. It feels like a good deed and good deeds are important. And I've been working in the kitchens at the school and I've perfected the art of icing *anything*. Even if it's moving. Especially if it's moving. I know that's quite a specific skill to have but I think it might come in useful."

In the distance, a train appeared on the horizon.

"We're trying to find Good Sister June," said Hanna. "She's gone missing and we're going to find her. Are you going to try and stop us?"

"No," said Gareth. He looked deeply hurt. "Good Sister June is one of my absolute favourite people in the entire world. I'd never stop you from helping her."

---

1 You will note here that this is not quite the exact way things happened and that was because Gareth was trying very hard to follow Good Sister Christine's instructions to the letter.

The train pulled into the station.

Calla took a step forward.

Edie said, "It is now or never!"

Hanna turned around to Gareth and said, "I believe you. Please will you come with us?"

And so he did.

OH I DO LIKE TO BE
BESIDE THE SEASIDE

When the train pulled into Filey, Edie was the first off and within seconds she had disappeared. They caught up to her at a small café just by the station exit where she had stopped to read the menu. She looked up when they got nearer. Her eyes were bright.

"Bacon sandwiches! An excellent idea! Gareth, my dear little jacket potato, I would like you to order three bacon sandwiches, please! And Calla and Hanna, you might want something for yourselves as well."

Hanna smiled when she saw the panicked expression on Gareth's face.[1] "Just ask for three bacon sandwiches in total," she told him. "And anything you want as well." She turned to the man who had come out to take their order. "I know this is going to seem a little bit odd but have you seen a nun recently? She would have come out of the station in the past few days."

"I don't know," said the man from the café. He pocketed his notebook and looked thoughtful. "We see a lot

---

1 If you look into the mirror and imagine yourself being given a Brussels Sprout Milkshake then you will have an idea of what this looked like.

of people. Lots of tourists. I wouldn't really know if one of them was a nun. What do they look like?"

"A little bit like a penguin," said Edie. "They wear black and white[1] and also have deeply noble expressions."[2]

The man shook his head. "No," he said, "nobody matching that description, no."

"That's okay," said Hanna. "If you do see somebody who looks like that today, we'll be back here this evening. You can tell us then."

After eating their bacon sandwiches, they headed off into the town. They walked down streets that were covered with bunting and packed with ice-cream shops until they reached a small memorial garden full of benches and bright, rowdy flowers. While Gareth and Edie went off into the nearby supermarket to make enquiries, Hanna and Calla went into the garden to wait for them. At the front of the garden was a small stone arch with a caption engraved on the top of it and Calla read the words out loud: *In honour of the men of Filey who died for their country in the two world wars."*

A list of names was engraved down each side of the arch. Hanna read the left-hand column first. This was a list of everybody who had died in the First World War: *S. Bertolini, C. Van Dam, G. Weisenreider.* There were so many names and a story behind each one. She turned to look at the second column which was for people who had died during the Second World War.

[1] What is black and white and red all over? A sunburnt penguin.
[2] This is because we are thinking Important Things About Cake.

And then at the top of the column, she saw something interesting: *George Bishop*.

She waited until Edie and Gareth had returned before pointing out the name. "George Bishop," she said. "Maybe he was related. Maybe he was Great-Aunt Lily and Georgia's dad. Maybe they decided to call one of the children after him. The dates would work out and that's the sort of thing people did back in the day."

Calla did some rapid mental arithmetic with her fingers and toes. "Yes," she said, "and it gives Great-Aunt Lily another connection to the area. It's a reason for her to be local. If she had family, then—"

"If she had family here, then why would Good Sister June not know about it?" said Edie. She bit down on a sausage roll that she had accidentally on purpose purchased from the supermarket. "I know every inch of my ancestors' lives for the past five hundred years and one day, I will tell you about how my great-great-great-great-great-great-grandfather tied the Gordian Knot—"

"Well, maybe the family wasn't always here. If her dad died during the war, then maybe Great-Aunt Lily had to go away for a while," said Calla, who was more familiar with grief than the others. Her father had died when she was only a few days old and visits to his grave had been a vital part of her childhood. "A lot of people run away from their sadness and just keep on running. If her dad *did* die in the war, then maybe Great-Aunt Lily and her sisters or whoever was in charge of them all had to go off and get a job or something. It's not easy to survive by yourself if you don't have money."[1]

Hanna rummaged in her bag and found the newspaper report of William Bishop's plans for Little Hampden. "Look. He's called William George Bishop. *George*. So if we're in the right area for him then maybe we're in the right area for her. We just need to keep asking questions. Somebody has to have heard of Great-Aunt Lily Bishop."

"You are all very professional," said Gareth with admiration. "I'm going to make you the best afternoon tea to keep your brains in top condition. I was thinking that we could have madeleines on the beach and freshly made lemonade and—"

It was a sentence that was destined to remain unfinished because the four of them had walked around the corner at the end of the street. This was not in itself a sentence-unfinishing sort of thing, but the thing that they saw around the corner was.

It was the sea.

And suddenly there was nothing else in the world other than that.

1 This was something Calla knew very well.

TAKE MY BREATH AWAY

Hanna had seen the sea before, of course, and ridden on ferries and gone on planes that had soared over the top of it, but that sea had been wild and cold and sharp and the sort of thing that left you with nightmares and the deep determination to not go anywhere near it. This sea was something so very different. It was still and warm and soft and endless. The waves glinted under the bright sunlight and when water reached the beach, the sand and the waves swirled together as if they were forming a potion and a spell about to be cast. And then it would slowly be pulled back out towards the horizon as the wave went out to begin all over again.

When she turned around to see where Calla and Edie were, they were already next to her. Without saying a word, Calla grabbed one of her hands and then Edie took the other and the three of them ran giddily down to the edge of the sand. They paused for a moment to twist out of their rucksacks, throwing them to Gareth, who gathered them to him like an enormous mother hen, before splashing forward and into the sea, up to their knees.

Hanna lifted up her arms as if she was trying to keep them dry, before she plunged them into the water, all the way up to her shoulders and then, unable to stop herself, she slid underwater, found the sand underneath her feet and then pushed out and up through a wave until she was back in the air and the wind was whipping all around her. She turned and saw Calla and Edie laughing as they splashed each other, while in the distance, Gareth was putting up a big, striped umbrella and laying out towels for them all to sit and dry on.

It was perfect, she thought with sudden, sharp joy, it was perfect.

And then she remembered the reason that she was there in the first place.

And that it wasn't anywhere near perfect, not at all.

Because Good Sister June was not there at her side.

FINDING OUT THE ANSWERS

The rest of that morning was devoted to research and if you have ever attended one of Edie's heartfelt midnight lectures on How To Research During A Crisis then you will know two things. The first is that research is a noble quest best achieved on a full stomach and the second is that you must have a base of operations. This is a fancy way of saying 'somewhere to put both yourselves and all of your stuff' and for the girls on that bright blue day, that place was the beach. One of them waited there with their bags while the others went off to ask questions at the café and buy prawn sandwiches for lunch, and then they'd swap with somebody else to go and talk to the people fishing at the edge of the harbour before calling in at all the little shops on their way back.

When Calla and Gareth went off to check Filey library, Hanna stayed on the beach. She curled up with the notebook and when Edie eventually came back from asking some passing tourists how they'd made their sandwiches, and also if they'd seen a woman who looked a little bit like a penguin, she handed her the newspapers.

"Do you want to look through these? There has to be something there that we're missing."

Edie nodded and stretched out on the towel next to her. She began to turn through the pages. "There are not many people I would do research for on a beach," she said, "but for Good Sister June, I shall."

Hanna turned back to the notebook. She liked the way it felt in her hand. It was as if Good Sister June was at her side. She could almost hear her talking to her. The only trouble was that she didn't know what she was saying.

She continued to read it until she came to a page with a picture of Georgia, Lily and Good Sister June. The three of them were sitting together on a small step outside a building and smiling broadly at whoever it was that had taken the picture.

Edie leant over. "Which one do you think is Good Sister June?"

"Her," said Hanna. She pointed at the girl on the far right-hand side. She had her knees hugged up to her chest and there was a dreamy expression of happiness on her face.

"Yes," said Edie. She studied the photo. "Of course. She looks as if she has eaten an entire Victoria sponge all in one go."

Hanna smiled and turned back to the notebook. She kept flicking through the pages until the writing and the drawing stopped and then suddenly she realized that she was wrong. There was still writing on one of the blank pages or, at least, there had been writing there once, a long time ago. The light on the beach was so bright that she could see it clearly for the very first time. The page was creased, the paper was marked where somebody had pressed in with a pencil, and there was the faint, faint shadow of writing.

She reached into her bag. She found her own pencil and then, very lightly, began to shade it over the markings. Now that she knew they were there, she could find them and make their outline clearer. And even when it wasn't completely clear, she could feel the indentations on the page. The way that the paper had been pressed down by the pencil. The mark of somebody writing, quite firmly, onto the paper. And now all that was left was a memory.

If only she could figure out what it all meant.

She sat up for a moment to give herself time to think. Edie had wandered off to ask some nearby tourists if they'd seen a nun and so, for the moment, Hanna was completely alone. And yet, she wasn't. She was surrounded by the sights and sounds of the seaside everywhere she looked. It was like an Enid Blyton book come to life. The sound of the waves. The call of the seagulls. The chatter of people as they passed her. Laughter. Noise. Life. Everything that was in the notebook was here.

She slid back down onto her elbows and picked up the notebook again. She turned the pages over and saw a cake that had been iced the precise colour of a seaside sunset; meringues teased into the precise shape of a white-topped wave as it hit the shore; and a picture of something called a candyfloss cake that was so real that she almost thought that the people walking past her were eating great slices of it already.

And then, as soft as the wind rolling in from the sea, she realized what she had been missing all along.

JUST ONE WISH

One day, back when she had been at the school for only a handful of months, Good Sister June had asked Hanna to help her reorganize the library.

"It wasn't always like this," she said, gesturing at the room about her. "And I don't think it always *should* be like this. Libraries should change because people change. So, I think it is time for us to reorganize our library."

Hanna had expected the reorganization to be a very adult and very dull affair because that was how things had always happened in the embassy. People would say they were going to do things, and then there would be a lot of pieces of paper and long, long meetings and occasionally somebody coming round to talk to her parents about Optimum Targets. She rapidly realized that this was not going to be the case for Good Sister June's reorganization.

The first thing that they did was take all of the books off the shelves and create an elaborate book fort down the middle of the library. They made an entrance big enough for Good Sister Paulette to get through and included a seat for Good Sister Gwendolyn to sit on and watch her films, and even a small table for Good Sister

Honey when she came up to the library with Hanna's supper. Good Sister June taught Hanna how to stack the books to make tall walls that would not break even if you leant on them and how to leave gaps wide enough for fairy lights to be threaded through and provide light for impromptu midnight feasts.

"The secret is poetry books," said Good Sister June. She picked up a handful of books from the nearest shelf and carefully began to stack them on one wall of the book fort. "They're small enough to allow you things like windows and *detail* but they're also sturdy enough that they don't collapse the moment that you look at them." When she had finished building the window, she poked at it in an experimental fashion and looked satisfied when it did not move one inch. "Ah! Engineering! A vital skill!"

"I've never read much poetry," said Hanna, who had been building a small seat out of Noel Streatfeild. "I don't think I've read any, actually." She put down her copy of *Ballet Shoes* and studied Good Sister June thoughtfully. "I don't think I really like it. It never makes sense to me. I don't understand it."

"That's because you've not read the right one," replied Good Sister June. "There is a poem out there for everybody and all you have to do is find it."

"Have you found yours?"

Good Sister June nodded. "Yes," she said. And then, in a slow and steady voice, she began to recite: *"The sea is calm tonight. The tide is full, the moon lies fair—"*

THE LIGHT GLEAMS

And then on the beach, with her finger tracing the ghost letters on the page, all those years later, Hanna recited the next two lines along with her.

> *"Upon the straits; on the French coast the light*
> *Gleams and is gone; the cliffs of England stand."*[1]

It was from a poem called "Dover Beach" by Matthew Arnold and she had forgotten it until now. But Good Sister June hadn't. She had written it in the notebook and she had spent so long planning a life with Georgia and Lily at her side and then it had all gone so very wrong.

Hanna had never thought that words could feel so lonely.

She took a deep breath. She put the notebook down and when all of the others came back to join her, she told them everything.

"Everything leads to the seaside. The notebook. The poem. The recipes, even. There's one here that's for a

---

1 If you would like to read the rest of this poem, then you should befriend your nearest librarian and ask them to help you find it. Once you have found a copy, I recommend that you then read it by an open window and a horizon full of promises.

candyfloss cake.[1] I don't even understand it but I know that it wouldn't work anywhere else than the seaside. We just have to find which bit of the seaside she—and Great-Aunt Lily—is in. She's trying to find her. Even in the notebook, she's trying to find her."

Calla sat down cross-legged on the towel beside her. She tucked her hair back behind her ears and looked thoughtful. "What I find weird is the fact that Good Sister June was planning for this whole other life and then never had it—or even tried to have it. My mum always knew exactly what she was going to be and then she went off and did it. Good Sister June just—didn't."

"*I* cannot even think of her as a child," said Edie. She folded the newspapers up and put them back inside her bag to stop them from blowing away. "I have been trying very hard but always I think of just a slightly smaller adult version of her."

Hanna sighed. For the first time since they had begun this adventure, a strange feeling of doubt had slid inside her heart. She could not explain why it was there or even what had prompted it, but she knew that it was there. And that she did not like it. "What if we don't find her?" she said eventually.

"It has only been a morning," said Edie softly. She wrapped an arm around Hanna's shoulder. "We just need to give it more time. I think that you are right. I think

[1] This recipe is important.

that Good Sister June is by the seaside but not, perhaps, by this bit of it?"

Calla nodded. "I even rang the journalist who wrote the story about William and he didn't know anything else about Great-Aunt Lily. And then when I tried to use your interrogation techniques, Edie, he just got *super* confused and I couldn't get any further information from him. It was a bit weird, actually. He just didn't want to speak about it at all."[1]

"So all we know is what he put in the article. Great-Aunt Lily is dying and she lives somewhere by the sea."

"Tell them about the festival," said Gareth in a helpful fashion.

"Oh!" said Calla. She brandished her phone at Edie and Hanna. "Food! Festival! Whitby!"

Edie leant forward and placed her hand on Calla's forehead. "Calla, my delightful little pineapple, I know that you're excited but I need you to make *actual* sentences."

Calla took a deep breath. "It's a festival," she said. "I saw the poster on the library door. There's a food festival in Whitby. It opens this evening for a sneak peek and then it's on for two days after that. If anybody's going to know about bakers and Great-Aunt Lily and maybe even Good Sister June, then I bet they're going to be there."

"Oh, I have trained you *so* well," said Edie.

Gareth nodded. "We can get a room in the youth hostel there and I can ask to use their kitchen and make us all

1 And in a few chapters, I shall tell you precisely why that is.

eggy bread for breakfast and eggy bread always tastes better at the seaside."

Hanna said, "But what if she's not at the festival?"

She did not want to say it but she knew that she had to.

"Oh, Hanna," said Calla, "you can't give up. We're going to find her."

"I'm not," replied Hanna. She took a deep breath. "I just—I don't know. I feel like the closer we get to her the farther she slips away."

Edie wrapped her other arm around Hanna and pulled her tight. "Hanna, my dear little *cochon d'Inde*, are you losing, perhaps, a tiny little bit of hope in our noble quest?"

"A little bit," replied Hanna. Her voice was quite muffled because she was currently being pushed firmly into Edie's shoulder. "Sorry."

"Good," said Edie. She released Hanna and rocked back onto her knees. "That means that now I can tell you about a man called Martin Luther King Jr.[1] He was *technically* American but you and I know that in his heart, he was really French. Anyway! He said that 'We must accept finite disappointment but never lose infinite hope' and what *that* means is that we must be open to being disappointed and to things going wrong but never, ever stop believing that they will work out for the better. Things

---

1 Whose favourite dessert was a pecan pie, and I know that this is not a cake but then, as Martin Luther King Jr was a Very Good Chap, I am going to allow it just this once.

go poorly—they always do—but our quest will succeed because we really are very good at this sort of thing."

"I second *all* of this," said Calla, who was rummaging in her bag. "Good Sister June wouldn't give up if one of us was missing and we won't give up on her. She's our family. Family stays together. Even when a bit of it thinks that it has to go off and sort out something by itself." She produced her train timetable and began to flick quickly through the pages. "Look, we can get a train to Whitby in an hour and then go to the food fair this evening and maybe tomorrow as well."

"Well then," said Edie. "We must go."

"I do like cake," said Gareth. He looked at the three girls and then longer at Hanna. "What do you think, Hanna? Do we continue?"

Hanna nodded. "Yes," she said. "Let's go get that train."

For there was another part of the poem, one that she had not shared with the others, and all of a sudden she had realized that it was Good Sister June telling her to continue.

Come to the window, sweet is the night-air!
Only, from the long line of spray
Where the sea meets the moon-blanched land,
Listen!

A BRIEF NOTE FROM
YOUR NARRATOR

I have been thinking for a while that I should tell you a little bit more about William Bishop and now seems like an excellent time to do so. This is because of three things:

1. You already know that he is not a good egg.
2. He is about to make things a lot worse for Edie's band of anti-kale revolutionaries.
3. But even people who are not good eggs who are about to make things a lot worse have a story.

And this is William's.

It begins with his great-grandmother meeting a boy and falling in love.

It was a love that surprised them both for it should not have happened. They were in the middle of the First World War and he was a soldier and she was a nurse and both of them were thousands of miles away from home when they found each other. But they did and they fell in love and for a moment everything was desperately and utterly perfect.

But moments do not last for long in such times and this was no exception.

Because William's great-grandmother's love was killed in a battle and so she went home. She could not understand how death could come so swiftly for somebody she loved so much and she spent many months trying to figure it out. She was only briefly distracted by the birth of her son, a wide-eyed and silent boy, and then the way he looked so much like her love sent her spiralling back into her sadness.

You might be wondering where her family was in this and so I shall tell you. They had disowned[1] her when they realized she was pregnant and that she had never married her love.[2] And so her name was forgotten by her family and when her sister had children of her own,[3] they never knew the name of their aunt. And when the wide-eyed and silent boy had children of his own and then grandchildren, they never knew the name of the family who had left them all alone.

There were other things that they never knew as well and it stemmed from that all-encompassing sadness of William's great-grandmother. She found herself living more and more inside her mind and in the memories of

1 Disowning somebody is when you ignore and reject any relationship or connection with them.
2 To disown someone for this reason is something especially horrific that people did many years ago and I cannot imagine how awful it must have been for the people that they did this to.
3 Whose names were Sarah, Georgia and Lily... Sound familiar?

the time she had spent with her love. She would relive the days that they had spent together and cook the food that they had eaten together and slowly but surely, the rest of her family began to do the same.

And even as the world changed and the years went by, their sad and lonely house stayed the same. They rationed their food out, just as William's great-grandmother had done during the war, and they ate meals that were faint memories of the days that had gone by so very long before. Food was not to be enjoyed. It was not even there to make you happy. It was to remind you of everything that you had lost.

It was no different for William. He grew up surrounded by cabbages and parsnips and turnips and when his school friends asked him to their birthday parties, he would stay at home with his family instead. And so he lost the few friends that he had and when his incomprehensibly old great-grandmother died, and then his grandmother a few days after that, he began to lose his family as well.

And after the death of his parents, he was all that was left.

Luckily enough, William was bright and smart and he managed to find a job that would pay the bills and give him time to figure out what he was going to do with himself. The only problem was that his job meant that he had to be part of the real world and he did not like it. It was too bright, too loud, and the food? It was horrific. There was too much choice. Too many flavours. Things had to be simpler. His family had been right all along. Food needed to be plain. Grey. Ordinary.

So William quit his job as soon as he could and spent his days trying to find a way to make this happen. A world without cake. It would be so beautiful. So much easier.

And one day, as he ate his kale soup in his dark and lonely house, he had an idea.

A kaley, pastey, sludgey sort of idea.

THE SOUND OF DRUMS

Now that you know a little bit more about William Bishop, it is time to tell you about Dominic Burton. Dominic was the Mayor of Little Hampden. He was a tall and red-faced individual who liked nothing better than telling people what to do and how to do it. He was also very fond of expensive things. He always ordered the most expensive meal in the restaurant and the most expensive drinks, and this was not because they were the *best* things to eat or the *nicest* things to drink but rather because he liked the way that ordering them made him feel. Money, for Dominic, was something to be shown off and so he spent it loudly and publicly.

And when he met William Bishop, the two of them had understood each other in the way that only not-particularly-pleasant individuals can.

William and Dominic always scheduled their meetings for very early in the morning. They were so early that the council offices were completely empty so that nobody ever saw Dominic sneaking in through the back door. William always made sure to park his car several streets away so that if anybody saw him, they would think that he was just about to go to the bakery, and both of them also turned off their phones so that nobody might be able to track them at a later date.[1]

"I'll be quick," said William as he shut the door behind him. "It's all going as planned but I'm not going to wait until I get the papers through for the property. My great-aunt will never know what we're up to with it. Even if she does figure it out, then it'll be too late. We'll have turned Little Hampden into the Kale Paste capital of the world and we'll have made a fortune. And you and I will do very well out of it, I promise."

Some of you might not quite understand what this speech of William's actually meant so I shall break it down for you. Papers are a fancy way of saying "the stuff that proves who owns what". The papers for the bakery were still with Great-Aunt Lily because she was still, officially, the owner. Yet William was so convinced that he was going to become the owner that he was going ahead with his plans to change it into a Kale Paste café. And the last line of his speech was a fancy way of saying "I am going to give you some money to help me make this happen" and the smile on Dominic's face was a fancy way of saying "Great plan, thank you very much".

This was not the first bribe that William had given out. He had bribed the local newspaper editors to run

1 You might be wondering how, if there was nobody around, I know about the contents of this chapter? The answer is that people do not like keeping secrets for long and even the people who do like keeping secrets will definitely not keep them for long when given a slice of Good Sister Honey's triple-layer chocolate fudge cake.

nothing but positive coverage about his plans to turn Little Hampden into the home of Kale Paste. This was why the newspapers had been so suddenly full of interviews with him and why reporters had been very reluctant to talk to small girls who were trying to get information from them.[1] He had also given bribes to the local radio stations to play nothing but vegetable-themed songs;[2] and to the local traffic warden to accidentally on purpose give tickets to anybody who stopped outside the ice-cream shop, and to the person who ran the traffic lights to turn them red for everybody who had gone to buy chips on the way home.

"There's just one more thing," said William to Dominic. "I want that school. We've been talking it over for too long. Things need to happen quicker. Those girls need to be gone. I need that building for my new Kale Paste factory so that I can increase production."

"You just need to give it a little while longer. Once you're selling Kale Paste and it's everywhere in the village, those girls won't want to stay here. It will get rid of them, I promise. They're obsessed with sugary treats. All they have in that building is cake."[3]

"Okay," said William.

1 Remember Calla's phone call earlier?
2 It was not proving popular with some of their listeners. You might even say that it was making them grum-pea.
3 This is a lie because there are also biscuits and once, when Good Sister Gwendolyn pressed the wrong button on the internet order, we had an entire attic that was full of nothing but cheese and onion crisps.

"Is that everything?" said Dominic, who was thinking about the very expensive car he was going to purchase with William's brand-new bribe.

"Yes," said William.

And so the meeting that had not happened ended and the two of them went their separate ways. Dominic headed up to his office to look busy for when everybody else arrived at work, while William went off to the bakery. His route there was deliberately complicated because he did not want people to know that he had just been to the council offices. He left the building by the back door before walking down a narrow alleyway full of bins and rubbish bags. He then climbed three walls and cut through several back yards before finally arriving on the same road as the bakery.

When he arrived there, he was whistling. He was feeling particularly happy with the state of the world that morning and the thought of bringing misfortune upon the school and potentially ruining the lives of everyone in it was making him feel even happier. Things were going well for him. Kale Paste was going to be a success.

And so, William continued to whistle as he brought up all the sweeties from the newsagent's and put them in the bin, and he continued to whistle as he offered free kale milkshake vouchers to the local retirement home, and he only stopped whistling when he finally arrived at the road where the bakery was.

Because the road was full of people.

THE CROWD

There were at least fifty people between William and the bakery and he could not work out why they were there in the first place. There were people in suits and others who looked like they were on holiday; mums with babies wrapped up in their arms, and couples clutching each other's hands. And all of them, rather strangely, were eating small yellow cupcakes.

William took a deep breath. He turned to one of the nearest people and said, "Excuse me," because this is the way that British people begin every sentence.[1]

"Don't I know you?" said the man. "I'm sure I know your face."

"No," said William shortly.[2] "What's going on?"

"They were being handed out," replied the man. "And I thought, you know, why don't I stop and have a bun? I haven't had time in weeks—"

"What did they cost?"

1 Edie insisted I put this in.
2 This is a fancy word for being very abrupt and blunt in your speech. If you would like to know what that sounds like, it is the sort of "no, thank you" that you might say when offered a bag of raisins instead of a bag of candyfloss.

"Nothing," said the man. "It was for free."

"Free cupcakes?"

The man nodded. "It's really *very* civic-minded."

William took a deep breath. If there was anything that he didn't like, other than food that tasted nice, it was things being given away for free. All that potential profit being given away for nothing. It was just wrong. It made the back of his neck tingle.

The man finished his cupcake and then looked hopefully in the direction of the bakery. "I thought this was going to be something to do with kale?" He looked back at William. "But it looks more like it's going to be re-opening as a bakery. The cupcakes are a publicity stunt for it and if the rest of the baking is as good as these, then they're going to make a fortune."

"They're not going to make a fortune," said William. "They won't make anything of the sort."

He left the conversation there and began to push his way towards the bakery. He passed more people carrying cupcakes and then, as he got deeper into the crowd, he came across people carrying doughnuts and meringues and even tiny blushing macarons which were the precise colour of a rose petal.

And then he saw the girls. They were moving through the crowd and offering people food from trays covered in blue-and-yellow gingham napkins. Another group of girls was standing around a small table that had been set up just by the bakery window. It was covered in another gingham napkin and packed with boxes full of food, and right in the middle, was a bunch of fresh flowers.

Every now and then a fresh tray of food would be taken out into the crowd before it was borne back, empty. The girls would then say things like, "The secret is a little pinch of salt in the icing," and, "We need to bring chocolate éclairs next time," and all of the other girls would nod as if it made sense to them and then refill the trays.

And then they all noticed him.

"Oh!" said the nearest first year. She gave William a bright and warm smile. "You do not have a cupcake! You *must* have a cupcake. We've spent all morning making them as part of our great and noble endeavours against the forces of darkness!"

"I don't want a cupcake," said William. "I want you all to leave."

"We can't," said another first year. "We're in the middle of elevenses."

"Oh, you will," said William. He looked left and then right. "Who's in charge?"

"Me," said another girl.

And her name was Rose Bastable.

THE BISHOP
AND THE ROSE

Here are some of the things that you need to know about Rose. She has been at the school for as long as Edie has and has attended all of her lectures on Passive Resistance and Making Good Trouble and passed with flying colours. She is also the fastest runner in the school and able to make excellent ham and cheese sandwiches under a variety of challenging conditions.[1]

And so, after she had replied to William, Rose knew exactly what to do. She looked pointedly at the first years and said, "There are people who don't have chocolate tarts and I think Good Sister Robin wants to teach you all a new verse of *The Red Sarafan*. I'll talk to Mr Bishop. Don't worry. It's all right."

"Yes," said William with delight. "Go. It's all right." The thought of talking to one girl rather than this group of tiny and cake-obsessed girls was much more satisfying to him. He was good at intimidating people when they

---

1 The girls had tested this one quiet winter's evening and discovered that Rose could make excellent sandwiches with one hand behind her back, her eyes closed, and upside down. They had made her a certificate.

were by themselves. It was one of the special skills on his CV.[1]

It was perhaps unsurprising that he did not enjoy what Rose did next. She put two fingers in her mouth and whistled twice. Almost immediately she was joined by a group of girls, taller than the first ones who had offered William a cupcake, and all of them possessed of Steely Stares. And even though William did not know their names, I do and so I shall tell you. Rose had been joined by Lucy Millais and Maisie Holloway and Sethi Gopal and Sabia Gopal and Ellen Beaufort and Eloise Taylor and all of the other girls who had been in the library with Edie and Hanna and Calla the night before.

Almost unconsciously William took a step back.

Rose smiled. "We should introduce ourselves. My name is Rose and these are my friends. We're all students at the School of the Good Sisters and you, we know, are William George Bishop. We've read all about your plans for the bakery and the village and we don't like them."

"I don't care," said William. "And also, you're blocking the access to my bakery."

"We're not blocking the entrance to anything," said Rose. "This is a public thoroughfare and I'm pretty sure that people are thoroughfaring through it right now. All

---

1 Along with driving through puddles and splashing people at the bus stop, and laughing at small children when their ice cream melted before they had a chance to eat it.

we're doing is giving away cake to people and also teaching them how to say nice things in Ukrainian."

"Ви робите чудові бутерброди," said Maisie in a Right On Cue fashion. "It means *you make lovely sandwiches*."

"Хороша робота,"[1] said Rose appreciatively. She turned back to William. "Look, we all know who you are and why you're here. It's fine for you to want people to eat your Kale Paste but they can also eat cake. It's not down to you to decide."

"Precisely," said Lucy Millais, who, as the daughter of a baker, was having a lot of heartfelt feelings about this entire situation.

"So what?" said William. "I'm just trying to do the best for the village. Kale Paste is the best thing that's happened here for years. If you can't see it, then that's not my problem. You can give people as many cupcakes as you want, but they're not going to do any good. Have your moment and do what you need to do. I don't care. But if you're here tomorrow, then I'll call the police and have you removed."

"The police won't remove us," said Sabia Gopal politely. "Mr Richardson is one of our very best friends and he actually trained us all how to protest and break the law while not actually breaking the law at all."[2]

1 "Good job."
2 Mr Harold Richardson has been the policeman and the fireman and the "help my kitten is stuck in a tree" man for Little Hampden for a long time and he has been a good friend of the school for all of that. We love him very much.

"It was a very interesting class," added Sethi Gopal. "Did you know, for example, that a riot is not actually a riot unless it involves twelve people?"

"I meant the other police," replied William, because Mr Richardson had been one of the few people to resist his bribes.[1] "Oh, look, I don't have time for this. I've heard you and you've had your moment and done your little cake thing, but enough. Go back to your school. While you still have it."

All of a sudden, the temperature changed. The girls stared at him.

"What?" said Rose blankly.

"I'm going to buy your school. It's all arranged."

"It is not," said Maisie, unable to stop herself.

William gave her a long and deeply irritating smile. "Are you sure? Maybe your teachers haven't told you yet. But trust me, it's happening. So go home. Now. And don't come back."

"No," said Rose. "We're not going anywhere. You don't understand. Whatever you throw at us, whatever you say or do, we're going to be here telling people that they have another option. They can say no to you. They can make their own choices. They can fight."

"Well, they'll lose," said William. "They'll lose everything."

---

1 This is a fancy way of saying that Mr Richardson had looked him straight in the eye and said, "I don't want anything to do with that sort of thing at all." And that is because he is a very good egg indeed.

ROSE'S TEXT

That afternoon, just as Calla and the girls headed back up to the station in Filey, they received a text from Rose Bastable. Calla read it out to the others and because I am a helpful sort, I shall reproduce the text here as well:

Hello, Calla. We have met the enemy! He is HORRIBLE but we can handle him. How is the search going? Good Sister Christine thinks you all have really bad flu so make sure you cough if she rings you (and make it convincing).[1] We have set up a rota of first years to pretend to be the three of you in your room if she looks through the door so don't worry about that. ALSO. I do not want to add pressure but the kale man is trying to buy our school and evict us so that he can turn it into a factory for his horrible Kale Paste. I think we can hold him back for a few days but after that, I'm not sure. You'd better find Good Sister June soon. Things don't look good here.

Edie said something very rude in French before turning to the others. "We have to go back. No! We cannot! But we must! And bring weapons!"

---

1 Good Sister Christine did not think this, of course, but she was quite happy for the girls to think that she thought this. I know this sentence has a lot of people thinking things in it, so here is a joke: why do nuns love Swiss cheese? Because it's holey.

"Good Sister Christine would never sell the school," said Calla.

"It's not up to her," said Hanna palely. "If he can convince the governors to sell, then maybe they might. You never know what adults will do."

They were almost at the station at this point. Calla pulled out her timetable and quickly began to turn the pages. "We're going to have to make a decision," she said. "The last train to Little Hampden is in ten minutes." She closed up the timetable. Her eyes were wide. "But we can't go back, can we? I really don't know. I don't want Rose to deal with all of this by herself."

"And she wouldn't want us to stop looking for Good Sister June," said Hanna, almost to herself. She didn't know what to do. They had to find Good Sister June. But they also had to protect the school. What was the point of finding one without the other to bring her home to?

But then she realized that the man in the café was coming out to meet them.

"Hello!" The man wiped his hands on his apron and smiled as the girls and Gareth gathered in front of him. "I've been looking for you lot all day. I've been telling my regulars about your visit and asking them to keep an eye out and then, one of them said that he might have seen a nun a few days ago. He wasn't sure so I got him to describe her and when he said that she looked a little bit like a penguin, I knew that I had to tell you."

Hanna stared at him. "Are you serious?"

She felt suddenly breathless with excitement.

He nodded and gestured at the station. "He said that she was on Platform One so that means she was getting a connection to somewhere further up the coast like Scarborough or Whitby or maybe even Robin Hood's Bay. Anywhere up to Saltburn because that's as far as those trains go."

Calla fired a rapid text off on her phone: *Good Sister June was seen at Filey Station a few days ago. We'll be back as soon as we can to help. And we'll bring her with us. More soon. Stay strong.*

Edie said, "Was she—did she look well fed? Like she had eaten? I cannot imagine what she might feel like if she had not eaten."

Hanna locked eyes with the man. "Thank you," she said, "you've been amazing. You don't know how important this is to us."

Good Sister June had been here, she thought. Right here. Just a few days ago.

There was no way that they would stop looking for her now.

"Well, I'm just so happy that I saw you," said the man. "Honestly, it was only good luck that I was talking to my regular about her and I wouldn't have done that unless I'd spoken to you all this morning. He said she seemed pretty normal, you know? She went over the bridge and just sat on a bench until her train came. And then when the train came, she was on it and away."

All of a sudden, they heard the sounds of the next train to Whitby arriving. As the other people on the platform started to pick up their belongings and move towards it, Calla handed the man a piece of paper.

"Thank you," she said. "If you see her again, please call me. This is my number. We won't be far away and wherever we are, we'll come straight here. If she looks like she's about to get on a train, then just offer her some Victoria sponge and then she won't go anywhere."[1]

The man nodded. "It's a deal," he said.

"Thank you!" said Hanna again. "Thank you!"

She took one of Edie's arms and Calla took the other. Gareth hoisted all of the bags onto his shoulder. The four of them got onto a particularly empty looking carriage and found empty seats, all together in one corner. While Calla was buying their tickets on her phone, Gareth handed out cheese and crackers, and the train slid slowly out of the station.

And once everybody had finished eating, Hanna placed the notebook on the table. "Now," she said, "let's go over what we know."

---

1 I need to point out that this method does not work on every nun but it does work very well on Good Sister June.

THE SECRET OF
PEANUT FUDGE

When they arrived in Whitby, Hanna led them through the town and up towards the youth hostel. It was on the top of the cliff, just next to the Abbey, and they got two rooms for the night.[1] They dropped their bags off before heading back down into the town. Calla had already worked out where they needed to go.

"The food fair is going to be in the old market hall tomorrow, so that's on this side of the harbour. If we get down there tonight, there might be people setting up and we can ask them questions. Remember, we don't just want sightings of Good Sister June. We want anything about Great-Aunt Lily Bishop as well."

They walked through slender cobbled streets which were packed full of tourists and past souvenir shops that sold everything from postcards through to buckets and spades. There was even an old-fashioned sweetshop which made Gareth squeak with excitement.

"All right," said Calla, "but be quick."

---

1 There was no other option for somebody who had read *Room 13* by Robert Swindells.

The three girls waited outside as Gareth headed in.[1] He emerged a few minutes later with bags packed full of fudge and rock and sweets that Hanna could not even name. All that was left in the shop was a slightly stunned owner who had never sold so many sweets all at once.

As the girls and Gareth turned round a corner, they suddenly discovered an alley that looked like it went to nowhere. Memories of reading *The Whitby Witches* by Robin Jarvis made Hanna investigate and her instinct was rewarded by the discovery of a small and suddenly wonderful beach. It was tucked into the edge of the cliff and had a long stone breakwater stretching out on one side into the sea, still covered in green seaweed from the high tide last night.

Hanna gestured over at the edge of the breakwater where a number of people were working on a boat. "Edie, you go with Calla and the two of you ask them about Good Sister June and Great-Aunt Lily. I'll talk to the people on the beach here." She had noticed several different groups of tourists walking slowly across the beach.

Calla and Edie nodded and headed to the boat. Gareth gave them several pieces of peanut fudge to sustain them for their endeavours before producing a stick of rock for himself. He waved happily at Hanna. "I have some lovely cinder toffee for when you're ready!"

[1] I feel it is important to note that the girls did not wait outside because they were uninterested in sweets but rather that Gareth and his overexcited twirling had left very little room for anybody else to join him inside the shop.

Once Hanna had chomped a satisfactory amount of toffee and put some in her pocket for emergencies, she went over to the first group of tourists. "Hello," she said, "do you mind if I ask you some questions? Have you got a second?"

"Is it for a school project?" said one member of the group.

"Yes," said Hanna, because it was always simpler to let grown-ups believe what they wanted to believe. "History. I'm trying to find a woman called Lily Bishop. She had something to do with a bakery in the area. Maybe in the fifties or the sixties. A long while ago now, anyway."

And also my school is under threat, she thought, *from a mad kale man, so it would be really helpful if you could be quick.*

Another member of the group shook their head. "Sorry. No. We're not from round here."

"I'm also looking for a nun. She's dressed in black and white and—"

"You're looking for a nun *and* a bishop?"

"Sort of but no," said Hanna. She took a deep breath and tried not to panic. "I mean, she might be a bishop now, I don't know, but I don't think she is?" And when that didn't work, she began to explain it all over again but then stopped. She wasn't going to find Good Sister June here. "It's okay," she said, "don't worry. Thanks for your help."

There had to be somebody here who could help, she thought. Or at least, somebody who would get to the point quicker. They didn't have time for this.

She was suddenly distracted from her thoughts by a small bird circling in the sky up above her. It was too small and too square to be a seagull and then, all of a sudden, she realized that she knew precisely what it was. It was a duck. A small and brown duck to be precise. *Mallardus Amazonica*. The very duck that Calla's mum had spent her life protecting. The very duck that she'd been kidnapped for and then escaped.[1]

After a few minutes had passed, it was joined by another bird. This wasn't a seagull either but it was something that Hanna also recognized. A Qvada duck, just like the one that lived with Edie's family in Paris. That duck's name was Henri and he was a guard duck who had helped them deal with one particularly persistent burglar.[2]

Hanna watched as the two ducks circled above the breakwater before riding the wind currents across the beach and back up to the top of the cliff. A part of her dimly knew that somehow she was looking for a third bird—an owl, she realized, with a sudden, sharp memory of a picture book that she had read with Good Sister June back when she'd just arrived in the school[3]—and when the owl did not show, and the two ducks twisted and disappeared behind a distant cloud, she found that she was having a tiny, Tiny Cry.

1 To find out more about this, you must read a book called *How To Be Brave*. It goes very well with a custard cream.
2 To find out more about this, you must read a book called *How To Be True*. It goes very well with a macaron.
3 *Owl Babies* by Martin Waddell.

She stood there until it was over, and then headed back to join Gareth. He smiled at her and produced two small paper bags. "Mint imperials or humbugs. Your choice."

Hanna took a mint imperial. She bumped Gareth with her arm. "I'm glad you're here."

When Calla and Edie came back, it was clear that they had News. They scrambled down the edge of the breakwater and then ran over to where Gareth and Hanna were sitting and practically skidded to a halt in front of them.

"Do you have news?" asked Hanna. She wiped her eyes.

"OH YES WE DO," said Edie in a capital letters tone of voice. "HOW COULD YOU TELL?"

Calla jerked her thumb at the boats. "One of the people down there—they take tourists out on trips—and a few days ago—he—!"

This might seem a strange way to finish her sentence but this was because she had run out of breath.

Gareth leant over and gave Calla a supportive sandwich. "It's ham and egg. Eat it once you've got your breath back. Not before."

"And *I* will take over the rest of the story while you do," said Edie, who had already devoured her own supportive sandwich.[1] "What Calla is trying to say is that the other day, one of the people who takes the tourists

1 Ham and cheese with an exquisitely sliced layer of gherkin.

out for trips had a woman on board who looked very much like a penguin. She was interested in some of the villages further up the coast and really interested in one called Rutherford Bay—she asked loads of questions about it—you can't get there unless it's by boat—and also the village next to it—and IT WAS HER. GOOD SISTER JUNE WAS HERE!"

"Hang on," said Hanna, leaning forward. "Rutherford Bay is mentioned in the notebook, yes, but we have to be sure. How do they know that it was her? Did she do anything in particular? Anything noteworthy?"

"Know this: they saw her sitting here—having her lunch—and she had a slice of VICTORIA SPONGE."

"Oh," said Hanna. "*Oh*."

"She has been here, Hanna, my favourite little buttercup, we are SO close!"

"We are very close but we *still* need more information," said Calla, who had now finished her sandwich and caught her breath. "They know that she came back to Whitby on their boat but she might have got on another boat the day after that. Logic would say that she's headed towards one of the villages that she was interested in, but there are so many that it could be. I got them to make me a list and we can cross-reference it against that list in the notebook when we're back in the room. Maybe we can even get them to give us a boat ride tomorrow, just like they did for her."

"You're right," said Hanna. She took a deep breath and tried to still the wild hope of her heart. "You *are* right.

We need more information. So let's go to the food fair and get it."

And so they left the beach behind and climbed back into town.

THE PERILS OF TURNIPS

Gareth was the first to find the fair. He paused in the middle of the street and sniffed the air. "This way," he said confidently. "The breeze holds the scent of icing sugar and just the gentlest sprinkle of roasted almonds." He led them towards a tall red building which was surrounded by vans and cars and people carrying boxes in and out of it. For a moment they stood and watched and it was only when Gareth let out a small squeak of over-excitement that Hanna realized that they might have a problem.

"Gareth, we have to get in and ask all these people about Great-Aunt Lily and Good Sister June. So you're going to have to control yourself and not get over-excited and make them throw us out."

"But the crispness of the pastry!" said Gareth as a particularly tempting tub full of sausage rolls passed him. "The sweetness of the custards!"

"Gareth," said Hanna again. "I need you to count to ten and take a deep breath."

"But the little butterfly buns with their tiny sponge wings!"

Edie gave him a look. "Gareth, my delightful friend, I will bash you on the head with a turnip if you don't calm down. I do not have a turnip to hand right now, but I swear by the spirit of storming the Bastille, I will find one."

"Here," said Calla. She gestured at a small bench, just by the door. "Sit there, Gareth, and don't move. Promise us you won't. We'll go inside and ask things and then come back and find you."

Once Gareth had been suitably settled onto the bench and Edie had given him another one of her severest looks, the three girls headed into the market hall. The room was packed with activity and life: in one corner, people were unpacking jams and honeys and soft, thick *focaccias* decorated with rosemary and flowers while in another, people were setting up stalls full of golden bread rolls and loafs dotted with sesame seeds. One wall had nothing but people selling biscuits and cake: iced cupcakes, laced with intricate patterns and designs, sat next to enormous four- and five-tier cakes, stacked one on top of the other with trails of flowers running from top to bottom, and next to them, rows and rows of cake pops lined up for people just to nibble as they walked around the room.

In a dreamy and rather distant tone of voice, Calla said, "It's perfect."

Edie nodded. "They are all so skilled and talented that I think they all must be French. There is no other way to explain such wonder. Perhaps our first question must be to ask them what they had for lunch today. It is the perfect way to figure out the French from the English. The English are gifted in many ways but in lunch, they are not."

"You can't ask them about lunch," said Hanna, even though she knew that it was a very important question to ask. She took a deep breath and focused. "Remember: we're here for Great-Aunt Lily and Good Sister June. You've got to find out about people who look a little bit like penguins and also old ladies who know a *lot* about cake. Ask anybody who's selling Victoria sponge if they've recently sold some to a nun."

Calla nodded and turned to the nearest stall where somebody was carefully unpacking cookies out of a box. "I'm sorry to bother you. We're looking for a nun. Have you seen her? We know that she's in the area and that she's been buying Victoria sponge."

Edie headed over towards another stall. "Hello," she said in her brightest and friendliest tone of voice. "I am from the local newspaper and because I am French and so, the only person at the paper with *any* taste, they have sent me to talk to people who make cake. Tell me the secret to your *Brazo de Reina* and also if you have, perhaps, seen a nun at all today?"

Hanna went over towards the chutneys but, alas, she was not destined to ask any questions at all. This was because she was distracted by a small commotion at the other side of the building. The commotion's name was Gareth and he had tried very hard to stay where the girls had told him to stay, but a tray full of freshly baked vanilla slices had completely distracted him. He had followed the bearer of the tray into the room and then accidentally tripped over a yet-to-be-unpacked box of chocolate chip brownies. It was at this point that Hanna had turned around, so she was just in time to witness Gareth slide along the floor and crash headfirst into a pile of empty cardboard boxes.

"Oh my goodness," said the woman at the stall next to her, who had also been watching this, "I hope he's all right."

And because Gareth was currently being helped to his feet by a crowd of people and also being given a Hope You Are Okay And Maybe This Will Make You Feel Better Slice Of Lemon Drizzle Cake, Hanna looked back at the woman and smiled. "Yes," she said, "he'll be okay."

And then Hanna did not say anything else because right there, in front of her, in the absolute centre of the woman's stall, was a cake that she'd only ever seen in one place before.

In the pages of Good Sister June's notebook.

A RECIPE FOR A CANDYFLOSS CAKE

INGREDIENTS:

Four ounces[1] *of butter*
Four ounces of caster sugar
Four ounces of flour
Two eggs
A pinch of salt
One bag of candyfloss
Icing sugar

METHOD:

Mix the butter, caster sugar and flour together. Fold in the eggs and a pinch of salt. Mix until fully combined. Separate the mixture out into two equal-sized tins and then bake until golden brown and slightly risen. The sponge should spring back lightly when you touch it with a finger.

---

1 Back before *grams* and *kilograms*, people used to measure things out in *ounces*, *pounds* and *stones*. Sixteen ounces made one pound and fourteen pounds made a stone. You might ask what a lot of stones then made, so I shall tell you this: they made lovely houses.

Once it's cool, prepare a substantial amount of butter icing. Spread both cakes with icing and then place a layer of candyfloss on the top of one layer. Then pick up the other cake and sandwich it on top of the candyfloss layer. You should have a layer of sponge, icing, candyfloss, icing, and then sponge so make sure you put the top layer on the right way round. Once you have done this, you can then ice the top and sides and decorate with the remaining candyfloss. And if there is any candyfloss left, then you must eat it.

(June—WE LOVE IT AND WE LOVE YOU. This cake shall be sold at Bishop & Mortimer every single day because it is PERFECT.)

DARE TO HOPE

"**Y**ou look like you've seen a ghost," said the woman. (It feels very impersonal to call her "the woman" so I shall call her Laura because that is her name.)

"No," said Hanna. "I've seen a cake." She gestured at the candyfloss cake. It looked exactly as it had in the notebook. The colours. The icing. Even the way that the candyfloss was twisted across the top of it and down the side.

"Oh! Well, it's a very unusual cake. No wonder it caught your eye."

"It's beautiful," said Hanna. "Did you bake it yourself?"

Laura nodded. "I bake everything. It was a bit of a squeeze for time though. I wasn't sure if the fair was going to run. They were trying to ban it and instead sell this weird vegetable paste thing? There was this guy going on about it and how you could make cakes out of it but I wasn't convinced."

Hanna took a deep breath. *William Bishop*, she thought, *he's been here.*

"And luckily enough I wasn't the only one who felt like that," said Laura. "They sent him packing and now we're open. And I'm glad we are! I've already sold more than I expected and we're not even properly open yet."

"And the candyfloss cake? Have you sold much of that?"

"Do you want some?"

Hanna nodded. "Yes, please," she said. She could not take her eyes off it.

"You've got good taste," said Laura as she wrapped up a piece. "Not many people make them or, if they do, they don't get it right. The secret is that it's got—"

"—a layer of candyfloss right in the middle, sandwiched between two layers of slightly salted butter icing," said Hanna.

Her heart was racing.

"How on earth do you know that?"

"My grandmother used to make it," said Hanna, even though her own grandmother had died long before she was born.

A curious expression passed over Laura's face. "Does your grandmother live locally? I'm only asking because I was taught the recipe for this by my mother who got taught by *her* mother who was taught by an old lady who lived nearby but I've never worked out who she was. I even went to the library to look up all the bakers and chefs in the area but I never came across any mention of the woman or her cake. All I could think was that she lived somewhere farther up the coast. There's some very remote villages nearby and some that you can only get to by the sea."

And at this point Laura paused.

"Do you know what though?" she said. "You're not the first person this week I've told this to. Only yesterday, there was this other woman asking about the candyfloss cake—she came to my bakery, I have one, just down the road, and when she saw it in the window, she stopped dead in her tracks. Honestly, I thought she was ill or something. Just stopped dead in her tracks before she came in to ask me about it. I told her exactly what I've told you. And before she left, she bought a slice of it to take with her and also some—"

"Victoria sponge," said Hanna.

"Yes," said Laura. Her eyes grew wide.

"And she was a nun," said Hanna. "Wasn't she?"

"Yes," said Laura.

Hope, thought Hanna. *Dare to have it. Particularly when it is right in front of you.*

"How on earth do you know all of this?"

"Because she's my friend and we're looking for her," said Hanna. "Will you tell me everything about her?"

"Yes," said Laura. "Of course, I will."

IN WHICH, A KETTLE

That evening, as Hanna, Calla, Edie and Gareth made their way back up to the youth hostel, they decided to have a conference call with the other girls back at Little Hampden and tell them everything that they had learnt. Calla's phone did not have any network in the room and so their call was accomplished by Edie climbing to the top of the youth hostel's roof and soldering a small wire to the TV aerial. She then threaded this through several more wires on the roof, splitting and crossing them with each other, before sliding back into the bedroom window and looking deeply satisfied with herself. "So! I have set it up so that we can radio the school and all I need to do is make us a receiver here now—perhaps, ah, yes! That kettle! Calla, if you please, will you hand it to me?"

Gareth sat down on the edge of the bed to watch. His eyes were wide. "Are you going to make the receiver out of that?"

"But no, my dear Gareth," said Edie. "I am going to wire everything into the receiver in my bag. The kettle is for the cup of tea that you are about to make me. Hanna—pass me that spatula?"

After a few minutes of hard work, she twirled a knob on the receiver and a low buzz of static filled the air.

"OH, I AM REMARKABLE! YES! INDEED! Oh, it thought that it would not work but it had not met me! Oh! Wait! Not you, Malcolm, I do not wish to speak to you although I do wish you the best in all your exploits! We must share tradecraft tips at some point! Let me retune my device a little—AH-HA! Everybody—come! I have done it! Yes, Rose, hello! Of course, I meant to tell you that I'd left a transmitter in your shoe but I did not! You must forgive me! We left school so swiftly that there simply was not enough time! And also, I am quite enjoying the idea of you hopping right now!"

"I thought we were being invaded by robots," said the Deeply Unimpressed voice of Rose Bastable. "There was all this beeping and flashing and then I started hearing somebody talk and then it was coming from my foot and when I realized it was you—"

"Honestly, what a treat, you are so very lucky," said Edie with serene indifference. "Rose, we have news on the search for the dear Good Sister June. Tell her everything, Hanna."

And so Hanna did and when she was finished, Rose said, "You'll be getting on a boat tomorrow then."

Calla nodded before realizing that nods did not necessarily translate well on the radio. "Yes," she said, "we're going to go back down to the harbour tomorrow morning, first thing, and get them to drop us off at a place called

211

Rutherford Bay. Hanna found it in the notebook with a list of other names so we'll start there."

"And we will return with Good Sister June in time to fight the kale man!" said Edie.

"Does he really want to take the school?" said Hanna.

"Yes," said Rose. "We're going down into the village tomorrow morning. We're going to get signatures for a petition against him and we have a little distraction planned for him as well. Trust me, we've got this sorted. All you need to do is concentrate on bringing Good Sister June home. We're going to need her. We can't lose the school. We can delay him for a while but if he wants to take it, then—well—he's an adult, and adults will always pay attention to other adults rather than listen to us."

"We'll find her," said Hanna. "Trust us."

"I do," said Rose. "Always."

"Good!" said Edie. "And now we must say *adieu*, for it is time for supper and then for us to sleep."

TO THE BOATS

The next morning, they found a man with a boat.[1] His name was Thomas and the boat's name was *The Nancy Blackett*[2] and when she saw this, Hanna knew that it was a sign. She told Thomas, "We're not duffers, I promise. We won't drown," and when he smiled back at her, she knew that he understood. He handed out lifejackets and then, when they were all ready, he took the boat out past the breakwaters on the edge of the harbour and then out into the open sea. The boat went in a straight line away from the bay until Hanna wondered if Thomas wasn't going to stop at all but then he swung *The Nancy Blackett* around in a big turn that threw up white-tinged surf into the air before they began to head up the edge of the coast. They went past villages which clung to the tops of cliffs and tiny golden beaches tucked into the edge of the world, and in the distance, somehow, a silvery grey curve of porpoises began to follow the path of their boat, rising and cutting

1 This is not a hard thing to do in a town on the coast but would, I think, be Slightly More Difficult elsewhere.
2 Boats like a "the" before their name, and honestly, I think it is a fun rule and I might adopt it myself.

through the water, before disappearing off into the horizon.

Hanna was sitting at one side of the boat and every now and then she would hold her arm out over the top of the water and let the wind and the spray whip it back to her side. Calla was sitting next to her, her arms wrapped protectively around her rucksack and her train timetable, while Edie was at the back, next to Thomas, and telling him everything about their quest. Gareth was perched at the front of the boat where, despite the rocking motion of the waves and the occasional firm gust of wind, he was currently making the most remarkable sandwiches.[1]

"You'll want to work your way up and down the coves then,"[2] said Thomas once Edie had finished. "I'll drop you up at Rutherford Bay first and if you need to stop the night, you can get a room there. There will be somebody who can take you on to the next village from there and so on. And if there isn't, you just give me a ring and I'll come and get you."

Calla leant forward and got him to put his number in her phone. "Thank you," she said as she sat back down. "And don't forget—if you see Good Sister June, ring us straight away. We'll come immediately."

---

1 Gareth has advised me that he considered making a four-course meal but couldn't figure out where to put the candelabra.

2 This is a fancy word for a bit of land that is sheltered by another curved bit of land around it. If that does not make sense, then I must apologize because it is clearly too long since I have had my last biscuit and the sugar withdrawal is kicking in.

"She's very lucky to have people like you looking for her," said Thomas. A curious expression passed over his face. "I don't really have anybody like that."

"You have us now," said Hanna.

"And we will *always* have sandwiches," said Edie.

When they arrived at Rutherford Bay, Thomas dropped them off at the end of a rundown looking pier. He could not stay there for long because the currents were already pulling *The Nancy Blackett* away and so, the moment that the last person was out of the boat, Thomas gave them a quick wave and a shy smile and then he was gone. The girls and Gareth waited until he had completely disappeared and then headed on up to the village.

Rutherford Bay was unlike anywhere else they had been before. It was barely one street wide with houses that were so small and narrow that they looked as if they had been added at the very last minute. Some of the houses had tiny front gardens, almost the size of two first years laid end to end, whilst others did not have anything and just opened out directly onto the street.

Hanna found herself holding her breath. Everything was so silent and still and it all felt a little bit strange. The paint was peeling on the houses and all of the curtains seemed to be suddenly pulled when they walked past. It was as if something sad and horrible had happened here and everything was still coming to terms with it. Even the buildings.

Edie was the first to say it. "I do not think that this will be a helpful village. All of the people that I have seen have looked at me as if I have three heads and all of the people who did not do that have pretended to be invisible. Quite poorly, I might add. Even the newest member of Good Sister Gwendolyn's camouflage class would be more convincing."

"Well, there must be somebody here who can help us," said Calla. "Thomas said we could get a room overnight if we needed to and I don't think he was lying. Also, I still have no reception so we're going to need to get to a landline or out of here somehow."

Hanna looked thoughtful. Every detective book she'd ever read had had a moment like this. When everything didn't make sense. All they had to do was work it out. "We need to figure out if this village has ever had a bakery or a baker working here. There has to be some connection otherwise the name wouldn't be in the notebook and Good Sister June wouldn't have been looking at it on her boat ride. There has to be something here. We have to go door to door and make people talk to us."

Edie clapped her hands together and stood up. "It is lucky then that I am a qualified detective[1] and I have led on several complex cases with the *gendarmerie* and they are *reserving* me a desk for when I am even more qualified in case I choose to work for them but perhaps I might choose a life of crime, I am not yet decided!"

[1] This is not a lie. She was a PIP Level 2 accredited detective. The PIP stands for Pretty Incredible Pâtisserie.

And with this, she headed back down into the village to knock purposefully upon the door of the first house she came across.

A SLIGHT CRISIS OF CONFIDENCE

Things, however, did not go well. When they called at houses where somebody did answer the door, the girls were greeted with deeply unhelpful things like, "You're looking for a woman who looks a bit like a penguin who might have been here but might not?" and, "You're looking for a bishop who's a baker?" and, worst of all, "Look, I'm going to phone your parents and ask if they know about what you're doing."

Hanna was the first to finish her questioning and waited for the others at the bottom of the hill. She was joined by Calla, who sat down beside her and gave her the sort of look you can only give one of your very best friends in the entire world.

"Are you all right?"

"Yes," said Hanna. "But also no."

Calla nodded. "Exactly. One man asked if my parents knew what I was doing here." She looked deeply disgusted. "I tell my mum everything I'm doing, every day."

"Adults can be the worst," said Hanna because this explained everything. She stared out at the sea. "What I don't understand is why Good Sister June would mention this place in the notebook. It doesn't make sense. I could see her being in Whitby and I could see her being in Filey, but not here." This was wilder, she thought, and dangerous. The beach was more stone and pebble than sand and the tideline was marked with a thick layer of dark green seaweed. It was the sort of place for smugglers and being trapped by high tides and for having adventures that bordered on the edge of being terrifying.

The creak of the pier announced the arrival of Edie, who sat down next to Calla, and Gareth, who sat down next to Hanna.

"I am deeply unimpressed," said Edie. "We have been through the entire village and nobody knows anything. I mention the name of Bishop and they shut the door. I talk of bakers and they look at me as if I am proposing that we fly to the moon together. If the dear Good Sister June was here then I hope she had a better experience than I am currently having."

"We're having a crisis of confidence," said Calla.

Edie wrinkled her nose in disgust. "Well, I dislike it with all my heart."

"We must be missing something," said Hanna. She watched a wave roll up underneath the pier and then fade away. "Maybe it wasn't always like this here. Places change. Maybe Good Sister June's friend was here and then she left. What we know is that Good Sister June was interested in the area. That she specifically asked questions about this village. That has to mean something."

"It means that I still have no phone reception and that means that we might have to stay here forever."

"Well, I have survival skills so I will be fine," said Edie. "My ancestor, Adélaïde Berger, once survived for three whole years by herself with nothing but her shoes for company and I have more than that already. I have my shoes and a tin of anchovies I have kept inside my socks. So! I shall be trapped here but at least, I shall have *hors d'oeuvres*."

Hanna did not hear Calla's reply because she was too busy watching the water beneath her feet. The sea pulled a little bit of her heart towards it every time she saw it and this, even with all its darkness and danger, was no exception. It made her feel like she could just get on a boat and go anywhere that the water took her. That she could sail to the edge of the horizon and see what lay beyond it.

And it was then that she saw it. A small boat coming towards Rutherford Bay. It was so low in the water and painted so dark that she almost missed it.

That was it, she thought, that was the hope.

She looked across at the others. They were still talking amongst themselves. They hadn't seen it.

She looked back at the boat. She couldn't work out where it was going. There weren't any houses over there. And then, all of a sudden, she realized that there was one. A small house, as grey as the cliff behind it, with a thumbprint of sand in front of it. Windows that looked out to the sea. A roof made of wood and walls thick with seaweed.

Somebody got out of the boat and pulled it up onto the sand. They disappeared into the house.

Hanna stood up. Without a word, she began to walk over.

THE HOPE

Hanna knocked on the door of the house. "Hello," she said, "I know you're in there. I saw your boat coming in. Please may I talk with you?"

The door did not open. All that she could hear was the woman moving around the house and the distant sounds of Calla and Edie and Gareth. They were now talking about supper and what they could make out of seaweed, sand and Edie's emergency tin of anchovies.[1]

Hanna knocked on the door one more time, her fingers brushing against sand-crusted wood. "Hello," she said, "Please can you help us?"

The door opened. A woman stood there. She had her hair pulled back from her face and a serious, unimpressed expression. "No boat rides today," she said, "You've missed the tide now. You'll have to wait six or seven hours at least."

"You give rides?"

The woman stared at her. "Not now," she said. She began to shut the door.

"Please," said Hanna, but it was too late. The door was already closed.

[1] Spoiler: not much.

Hanna exhaled and took a step back. She walked over to where the woman had dragged her boat up onto the sand and ran her hand along the side of it. She could almost still feel the rhythm of the sea inside it. The wood held the memory of the water, just like her books held the memory of the readers inside of them. This boat felt like it had done a lot. It felt steady and safe. It had two long benches across the middle of it where people could sit. There was even a mark on the benches where people had used them as steps to get in and out of the boat. The wood had been polished from all of the feet that had walked across it.

She glanced back at the house. There was no movement but she knew that she was being watched. The woman looked like the sort of person who would notice everything happening around her, for miles maybe. But she was not stopping her from looking at the boat, at least, not yet, and so Hanna continued her gentle exploration. She was not sure what she was looking for but there had to be something. There wasn't anywhere else for the something to be.

And then she found it. A pile of crumbs on the side of the boat.

She leant over and picked up one with her finger and thumb. *Fresh*, she thought. *And familiar, too.*

She sniffed it.

Victoria sponge.

THE FINAL GUARDIAN

Hanna marched back up to the front door of the cottage. She rapped loudly on the front door. "Hello," she said, "I know you can hear me. I know you're listening." It was a small building, barely a room wide. There was no way that the woman couldn't hear her. "I know you've had a nun in your boat recently. And that you've taken her somewhere in particular. She's our friend. She's very important to us. She went missing and we've been trying to find her." She paused for breath. "Look—I'm not going to leave until you talk to us. And when my friends get here, they won't leave either. We'll just stay here and knock on your door until you tell us."

The door suddenly swung open.

Startled, Hanna took a step back.[1]

"Who are you?" said the woman. "Why are you here?"

Hanna took a deep breath. "Well, my name is Hanna and I'm here to ask you about my friend, like I said. She's a nun and I think you've had her in your boat very

[1] In the distance, Edie running towards her: "BE STRONG, HANNA, WE ARE COMING."

recently. There's—we've been following clues and they brought us here. I think she came here as well. She's been trying to find an old friend who lived around here or nearby. Somebody who baked. They have this recipe for candyfloss cake and—"

"There's no cake in Rutherford Bay," said the woman.

"Come on," said Hanna, unable to stop herself. "There has to be cake somewhere."

"Who sent you?"

"What? Nobody."

"Well you go back and tell that *nobody* that I've not done anything wrong."

Hanna stared at her. "I literally don't have a clue what you're on about."

"I'm on about somebody called William Bishop," said the woman. Her face was marked with a sudden disgust. "You're not something to do with him?"

"No," said Hanna. "Are you?"

"No," said the woman. "I hate him. He tried to ruin my business and take my home from me."

The two of them stared at each other.

"I hate him as well," said Hanna. "He's trying to ruin my village and take my school and replace it all with Kale Paste and my friends are trying to stop him and we're here trying to find our other friend who's gone missing and I think the longer it takes us to find her, the more he might actually succeed." She pulled out the notebook and brandished it at the woman. "All she left us was this and I think you gave her a boat ride, and all I need to know is where you took her and if you can take us there as well and I do not have time for *any of this.*"

"Well," said the woman. "You'd better come on in."

THE ENEMY OF MY
ENEMY IS MY FRIEND

The woman's name was Meredith Taylor and she had lived by the sea all her life. "My family have been here for generations," she said. "I was on a boat before I could walk. There's not a part of this coast that I don't know. All of the nooks and crannies. I was born by the sea and it'll have my bones when I die."

Hanna hugged her knees to her chest. Everything that Meredith said felt like a spell to her. A part of this was down to the house, and the way that it seemed to be built from the sea and the cliff and the sky, but another part of her knew that it was down to Meredith herself. The woman was like something out of one of her stories. She was so tall and so strong and so solid that she was almost like a tree, growing in the middle of the room. She could look Gareth straight in the eye and did, often, as she spoke. And sometimes, for reasons that Hanna could not yet quite understand, she did not say anything at all and instead just studied him as though she had never quite seen anybody like him before.[1]

---

1 Gareth, you will be interested to note, had not taken his eyes off Meredith since they had met her.

"Your life is so very unbearably romantic," said Edie in a breathlessly admiring sort of fashion. She was sitting next to Calla, the two of them perched on the edge of a bench that had been made out of a crate and something that looked rather like a barrel. If you squinted, you could see the panels of the wood and the long nails that carefully held them together.

Meredith smiled. It was clearly something she was not particularly used to. Her face seemed unsure, tentative, until all of a sudden she figured it out. "Well, your quest is unbearably romantic to me. I'll give you all the help that I can in finding your Good Sister June. I took her to a place called Merlin Cove. I don't take people there very often. It's hard to get to. We have to wait until the tide is just right otherwise it's pretty hazardous."

Calla looked suddenly concerned. "How hazardous?"

"Like a seven out of ten," said Meredith in a casual and not particularly comforting fashion.[1] "I was a bit worried about dropping her off there if I'm honest. It's very remote. I know there are a few houses there but I've never known who lived in them. It's not somewhere people go to be found. I only discovered it by accident myself. I was a bit concerned, really, when she told me that she wanted to go there but she persuaded me. She said that she'd heard the name a long while ago and wanted to find out what it was actually like. She persuaded me to leave her there as well. It felt all sorts of wrong, you know, abandoning an actual *nun* somewhere."

1 Calla, faintly: "I am not comforted."

"Good Sister June will be *fine*," said Edie with confidence. "She is a most remarkable woman. Once upon a time when we were snowed in at the school, she taught us how to make skis out of nothing more than a stale baguette and a broomstick."

Hanna leant forward with a question. "Meredith, did you think Good Sister June was something to do with *that man* as well? How did you know that she wasn't?"

"Ah," said Meredith. She smiled. "She was carrying cake."

TO THE MOONLIT SKY

They stayed in the small cottage beside the sea that night. Meredith cooked them all jacket potatoes for supper topped with nothing but lashings of butter and salt and they were the most delicious thing that the girls had ever tasted. Once they had finished, Gareth tidied up while she gave the girls blankets and cushions and helped them to make beds up on the floor, just next to the still-warm oven.

Calla was asleep within minutes and Edie was not far behind, despite her feverish promises to stay awake.

"I have not told you about my ancestors," she said to Meredith. "You must hear about their exploits upon the high seas. Do you know of Jacquotte Delahaye? And what about my Great-Great-Auntie Claudette who invented the jellyfish—" And then she did not say anything else because her eyes were closed and she was contentedly snoring.

Gareth made his bed by the front door. Meredith offered him the deep, comfy armchair in the corner of the room, but he was insistent.

"I have to keep an eye on everybody and make sure they're safe," he said. Within seconds he was asleep as well.

Hanna, though, did not sleep. It was not that she was uncomfortable because this was, she thought, like the very best sort of camping. It was because she had too many thoughts inside her head. She was thinking about Good Sister June being out there at Merlin Cove and what might have happened to her, and about Little Hampden and William Bishop and about how Rose might be feeling, being in charge of the protest without Edie at her side, and above all of that, about what she might say to Good Sister June when they finally saw her. A part of her wanted to tell her how much she loved her and about how they'd fight her sadness together, but another part of her did not even want to talk to her at all.

She sighed. It was all too complicated to know where to begin. She rolled over and tried to find a comfier position. She even tried to read her copy of *Eustacia Goes to the Chalet School* in the moonlight but nothing worked. She couldn't concentrate. It was only when she turned over again that she realized that she was not the only one still awake. Meredith was standing by a window with her hands wrapped around a mug. Their eyes met. "Can't sleep?"

Hanna nodded.

Meredith opened the back door and gestured for Hanna to follow her.

There was a full moon and the beach was bright and still. Every now and then a wave would roll up the sand, almost to touch Hanna's bare feet, before sliding back away from her. She watched it and then, almost hypnotized, found herself walking forward to greet the next. The water came up to her ankles. She gasped with the sudden, sharp chill of it. She stepped back and rubbed her feet to get them warm. And then she went into the water all over again because it made her feel alive in a way she could not quite understand.

When she looked at Meredith, she realized that the older woman understood. All of it.

"There are blankets in the boat," said Meredith. She turned to go back into the cottage. "You're welcome to sleep out here if you like. You'll be warm enough."

"I won't be able to sleep out here," said Hanna. Everything here made her heart and her head race. She wanted to float on her back in the water and look up at the moon. She wanted to count the stars and discover their names.

"You will," said Meredith. She turned around and headed back inside. "And even if you don't, then you'll be somewhere safe. If you need me, I'm inside. But you won't. You're not that sort of person."

And all of a sudden, Hanna was alone on the moonlit beach.

She went over to the boat to get one of the blankets that Meredith had talked about. She found them in a big tin box tucked underneath one of the benches, next to a pile of life jackets and a twist of sea-soaked rope. She picked one of the blankets at random and wrapped it around her shoulders. It was then that she saw the name of the boat.

"*Moonacre*," she said out loud, and traced her fingers along the worn writing.

Tomorrow this boat would take them to find Good Sister June and Great-Aunt Lily and everything would go back to normal, she thought. They would head back to school together and get back to the library and the North Tower. A part of her was looking forward to it and yet another part of her did not want it to end. The sea and the sky were part of her now. She felt it deep inside of her. It would be almost impossible to leave behind.

And it was then that she realized that Good Sister June might not want to come home after all.

A BRIEF NOTE FROM
YOUR NARRATOR

It is time to leave Hanna in the moonlight and return to Little Hampden for a while. We will come back to her, I promise, because she is about to—

No. Spoilers.

I'll tell you all about *that* shortly.

Because first of all, I need to tell you all about the day's events in Little Hampden.

On the same morning that Hanna and the others had got on the boat to go to Rutherford Bay, Rose had marshalled her troops and taken them once more down to the village to save it from being turned into an apocalyptic wasteland full of sadness and no cakes whatsoever.

They had attracted a lot of attention as they marched down the road and this was because they were carrying banners, which said things like "SOS! SAVE OUR STRUDEL!" and "MAKE BUNS NOT AGGRESSIVE BUSINESS PRACTICES" and "LIBERTY, PEACE AND AFTERNOON TEA", and also singing a hearty song of revolution which had been composed by Good Sister Robin for the occasion.

As the girls entered Little Hampden, they split up. Maisie Holloway and Lucy Millais and a group of pen-wielding first years headed off to the retirement home and the library and everywhere in between to pick up signatures for the We Are Not Particularly Happy about Mr Bishop Making Everybody Eat Kale, Please Can We Have the Bakery Back? petition. Sethi and Sabia Gopal took another group of first years down to the corner shop which was rumoured to be selling doughnuts and so would need defending from attack and also possibly the accidentally-on-purpose purchasing of their entire stock.

Rose took a moment to gather her own troops together. She had been joined by Eloise Taylor, Jia Liu and Sally Campbell and a numerous amount of first years.[1]

"Are we ready?" said Rose.

The nearest first year brandished a spatula at her in a positive if slightly incoherent fashion.

Another first year broke into a rabble-rousing song.[2]

Jia Liu decided to provide Rose with an actual response. "But of course," she said. "I have been waiting my entire life for this moment."

"Perfect," said Rose with a small, proud grin. "Come on."

---

1 First years do tend to go anywhere they want to go because they are so small and numerous that nobody can quite stop them. Not that you would want to, of course, because they are very useful in an emergency.
2 Unlike Good Sister Robin's song, this one had no lyrics and was really just more about Heartfelt Spirit.

THE FIRST OF SEVERAL
QUITE GRUMPY
PHONE CALLS

At that very moment in time, William Bishop was completely unaware of the revolution that was fermenting in the streets of Little Hampden. He was, instead, sitting in his car outside of the bakery and making a phone call to a man named Stuart Simpson. Stuart was the newest recruit to Little Hampden's police force and he was very fond of taking bribes and yelling at small girls.

"I need you at the bakery," said William. "Meet me there as soon as you can. You might need to be with me for a while. I think I'm going to have another visit from those awful girls. I'm going to need you to make them go away."

"I'll be there in about an hour. It's the earliest I can get there without rousing any suspicion from the old man."[1]

"Not good enough. I've paid you enough to get you here earlier."

Stuart shrugged.[2] "I can't."

---

1 The "old man" was not Thomas's dad but rather a man named Harold Richardson and you shall meet him shortly.
2 I know he was on the phone but I think that sometimes you can *hear* a shrug and this was one of those moments.

"Fine," said William. "But when you do get here, I'm going to need you to earn your keep and get rid of them. Those girls think that they're important and they're not. I've got three MBAs¹ and I run an enormous number of successful businesses. I don't have time for any of this. I'm going to take their school and they're going to regret even trying to stop me."

There was a long pause.

"That was a lot to take in," said Stuart. "Would you go over it again?"

"No," said William. He hung up and got out of his car and headed over to the bakery. There were no girls here yet but they would come. He could feel it. But for now, he was alone.

And the bakery was all his.

He had waited so long for this moment. His Great-Aunt Lily had never done anything *useful* with the property but he would. It would be the centre of his Kale Paste empire and it would make him money as soon as every rival eatery or cake shop had been driven out of town by the new restrictions. He'd tried to get Lily to give it to him before but she'd always made excuses. They never made sense. She'd talk about dreams and plans and when he'd point out that *he* had plans for it, she would look at him and shake her head. "No," she'd say, "not like that. You don't understand."

---

1 This is a qualification. The letters stand for "Master of Business Administration" and not, as you might imagine, "Maybe a Bit Annoying".

"Well, Great-Aunt Lily," said William as he stood before the bakery and unlocked the door.[1] "I understand completely now. I had the brains and the vision and you just couldn't cope with it."

He went inside to make plans. He was going to get rid of the dusty shelves and the counter display and he wanted to remove the long-forgotten display cabinet where Sarah had so long ago sold her bread and sweet sugary pastries. "I'll get rid of it all. You will be so brand new and beautiful and *modern*. I'll paint the walls green and the floor green and it will be the most beautiful thing that I have ever seen."[2]

And then he saw something outside of the bakery window that made him stop thinking about anything at all.

[1] You might wonder how he got the key and that was because he went on at Lily for a very long time until she could not bear it any more and gave it to him. And then, she—no, wait. You only have a few more chapters to go before you learn all about that.

[2] And also, as Edie has pointed out with some justification, curiously reminiscent of a bogey.

THE DANGLING SKILLS
OF ELOISE TAYLOR

That something was, in fact, somebody who you and I know as Eloise Taylor: the Best Dangler in the entire School of the Good Sisters.

William, however, only knew her as the girl who was slowly descending into view outside the bakery window. First came her head and then her shoulders and her waist and then her legs until all of her was dangling outside the window, completely upside down, and of all things, eating an apple pie.

William made a sound that sounded something like, "Whyph?"

It was then that the breeze began to twirl Eloise on the end of her rope. This did not stop her from eating the rest of her apple pie because she was a professional at dangling and also quite hungry. As she completed an entire rotation of dangling, she took her final bite of the pie and made direct eye contact with William. She then waved and, because she was quite enjoying the whole escapade, also gave him a thumbs up[1] as she was gently

---

1 Or a thumbs down, considering on your perspective.

lowered out of sight. The last thing to disappear were her ankles and then her feet and when these had completely gone, William suddenly realized what had happened.

He leapt towards the front door and flung it open. His mouth opened to yell Quite Rude Things.[1]

But there was nothing and nobody there, save an empty park bench[2] and the distant figures of people on their morning errands.

William took a deep breath. He headed back inside the bakery. He began to think, once more, about its refurbishment. He found it all very calming. There was one wall that would be just perfect for stacking the kale up against.

"That's better," he said out loud.

But then the Next Thing happened.

The Next Thing was another small girl who was, somehow, dangling at the bakery window. You and I know this small girl as Sally Campbell, Queen of Good Sister Gwendolyn's camouflage class, but William knew her only as somebody who was somehow spinning in mid-air outside his bakery window in a manner very reminiscent of an acrobat.

An acrobat who was also eating a flapjack.

When she realized that she had been noticed, Sally gave him a happy little wave. And because she was also

[1] "PARSNIP SANDWICHES!"
[2] Who was giggling quite quietly to herself at the success of her dangling.

very appreciative of excellent flapjacks, she pointed at her flapjack and shouted, "The secret is golden syrup!"

William made a sound that sounded something like, "Whyphsidugh!"

He hurtled forward towards the bakery door. He flung it open. He opened his mouth to yell several Very Abusive and Deeply Inappropriate Things.[1]

But there was nothing and nobody there except two park benches,[2] and the distant figures of people on their morning errands.

William took a very deep breath. He went back inside. He pulled out his tape measure and began to measure the wall. He began to take down notes. But between you and me, he was not concentrating on what he was doing at all. He was actually working his way around to the front of the bakery so that when the next girl arrived, all he would have to do would be to throw the door open and grab the perpetrator where she dangled. When he grabbed them, he told himself, he would make them regret all of their life choices and if that was not enough, then he would also insult their socks.

All of a sudden, somebody knocked on the door.

William took a deep breath.

They knocked again.

William put down his measurements.

---

1 "CABBAGE CUPCAKES! KIPPER MILKSHAKES!"
2 Who were now trying very hard to not look at each other in case they laughed.

The person knocked on the door for a third time.

William burst into action. He flung the door open and ran straight outside yelling, "I'VE CAUGHT YOU NOW."

The only problem was that he had not caught one of the girls.

He had, in fact, caught a very tall and very substantial policeman.

THE POWER OF MOMENTUM

It may not surprise you to learn that the momentum of a grown man running at a very angry speed into a policeman results in both of them crashing down to the floor in a rather eye-catching and noteworthy manner. It was so eye-catching and noteworthy, in fact, that Sally Campbell and Eloise Taylor completely forgot that they were meant to be disguised as benches and collapsed into hysterical laughter while Rose and the others on the top of the bakery[1] completely forgot that they were meant to be Invisible and instead hung over the edge of the roof so that they could see every inch of what was to follow.

Luckily enough William Bishop did not see any of this because he was too busy disentangling himself from the deeply confused and very much horizontal policeman.

"Hello," said William.

"Hello," said Stuart Simpson. "Do you greet everybody like this?"

"No," said William, "of course I don't."

As he stood up and brushed the dust off himself, he noticed that the two park benches opposite the shop had

---

[1] From where they had dangled both Sally and Eloise.

somehow disappeared. He was going mad, he thought. Furniture did not simply move. Clearly, neither bench had actually been there in the first place. He had imagined it all. Those girls were making him lose his mind. He had to keep his eyes on the prize. The bakery. The profits. The entire village eating nothing but Kale Paste. There, he thought. Perfect.

"You've not said anything for a while," said Stuart. "Are you all right?"

"Of course, I'm fine," said William. "What are you doing here?"

"You phoned me and asked me to come," said Stuart, who was feeling increasingly confused about this whole affair. He paused. "And then you sort of... assaulted me?"

"I thought you were somebody else," said William. "I've had people *dangling*."

"Okay," said Stuart. He paused and then, in a helpful fashion said, "Well, I'm not dangling."

"I *know* that," replied William. He bent down to pick a piece of paper up off the floor and handed it over to Stuart. "I think you dropped this. It's not mine."

"It's nothing to do with me. Maybe the postman's been," said Stuart, who was, after all, a policeman and rather good at figuring things out. "It looks like a letter. You should open it."

William glared at him. "I know how letters work." He opened the small envelope. Inside was a note. It read: *This is only the beginning.*

He said something very rude[1] and stormed back inside the bakery.

And up on the roof, Rose smiled with satisfaction. She turned around to the first years behind her. "Signal Maisie and Lucy. Tell them it's time to begin phase two."

[1] "RAISIN BROWNIES."

PHASE TWO

Phase two was a man called Mr Harold Richardson and only a few months ago, he had been all that Little Hampden had needed in terms of emergency services. He had run the police department singlehandedly, driven the fire engine when it needed to be driven, and even picked up enough first aid to successfully deliver three babies, two litters of puppies, and the unexpected foal of a Shetland pony who had been keeping secrets from everybody.[1]

All of this had changed when he had met the newly elected Mayor of Little Hampden. It had not gone well. Dominic Burton had been deeply unimpressed with everything that Harold had ever done, was doing, and might potentially do in the future. He had said things like Perhaps Harold Was Too Old and Clearly Not In Touch and Perhaps He Might Even Think About Retiring? and when Harold had disagreed with all of these remarkably capitalized sentiments, Dominic had disappeared before reappearing with a man at his side.

---

[1] The Shetland pony's name was Wollstonecraft and the foal was named Shelley and if you are ever in Little Hampden then you must remember to bring a carrot for them.

The man had offered Harold a rather enormous amount of money.

"Consider it a donation towards your retirement," said the man.

"What's your name?" said Harold.

"I can't tell you," said the man whose name did, in fact, rhyme with Schmillian Schmishop.

"Well, why do you want to give me money?"

"It's a donation towards your retirement."

"I'm not retiring."

"Then it's a donation towards you and your wellbeing until you do," said the man. "All I ask is that you'll do a few things for me in the future to say thank you."

"So it's a bribe," said Harold.

"It's a *donation*," said Dominic, who had been deliberately looking the other way throughout this entire conversation.

Harold shook his head. "This is a bribe and I don't want anything to do with that sort of thing at all."

The man looked at Dominic.

Dominic nodded before he turned to Harold. "Harold, my dear friend, I think it's about time that you started to take things a little bit easier. How would you feel if we hired somebody to help you deal with the mean streets of Little Hampden?"

The streets of Little Hampden were not particularly mean. If anything, they were gentle and really quite nice. They involved things like helping kittens down from trees and cutting the ribbon for summer fêtes. Admittedly there had been that one time Harold had had to arrest the Headmistress at the school but she had been a Bad Egg and he had found the whole experience rather thrilling if he was quite honest.[1]

"Well," said Harold, "I don't think I'd like that at all. I'm managing very well."

"Oh no," said Dominic, still with that horrible, hammy smile of his. "I don't think you are. We need a policeman who's more... *persuadable.*"

And so began the darkest time of Harold's career. Dominic hired a policeman called Stuart Simpson who thoroughly enjoyed being bribed and the two of them began to slowly stop Harold Richardson from doing the job that he had loved for years. They would give him the broken radio so that he had to stay inside the police station and get it fixed and whenever people asked for him to come and help them with their problems, Stuart would go off instead. And when it came to Christmas, a time when the villagers of Little Hampden would normally drop off chocolates as a thank you for all of Harold's hard work over the year, it turned out that the Mayor had banned all sugary treats from council-owned property so that all that Harold got were apologetic whispers and promises of chocolate once all of this was over.

It was because of all of this that Harold now rarely left the police station. He would spend his time lining up all of the pieces of paper on his desk, polishing the leaves on

[1] You can read all about this in a book called *How To Be Brave.*

his pot plant,[1] and making sure that all of his pencils were sharpened to an equal length. Sometimes he could make this last all day but usually it lasted only a few minutes and he would spend the rest of the day staring into the distance and wondering how to get his old life back.

And so, when Maisie Holloway and Lucy Millais and a group of first years came loudly into the police station, you will not be surprised to know that Harold almost fell off his chair with shock.

"Girls!" he said, as he pulled himself up from the floor. "Hello! Do you perhaps have a complicated situation for me to deal with? Or can we go over some basic legal training? Maybe we could chat about what to say when somebody wants to arrest you?"

Maisie waved at him and pushed a petition over the desk towards him. "Mr Richardson, how are you? We miss you! Will you sign our petition?"

He picked up the pen and then paused. "What's it for?"[2]

"We're protesting against that awful kale man," said Lucy. "And all of the things that he's trying to do to the village. He's being so mean to everybody and we're fighting back."

Harold put his signature on the bottom of the page.

"OUR FIGHT MIGHT POTENTIALLY INVOLVE OUR NOBLE DEATHS," said a first year,

1 His pot plant was called Simon. Simon enjoyed long walks on the beach, candlelit dinners and sitting beside an open fire.
2 This is something you should ask every time somebody wants you to sign anything.

from somewhere around Maisie's ankles. "AND IF IT DOES, WE ARE QUITE READY FOR THAT."

"IF NOT OUR DEATHS, THEN AT LEAST IT WILL REQUIRE A LIFELONG FEUD," said another first year, from just underneath Lucy's elbow. "AND HOPEFULLY THE SORT OF FEUD THAT INVOLVES BLUE CHEESE BEING THROWN SURREPTITIOUSLY AT PEOPLE."

"WE DO NOT LIKE BLUE CHEESE," said another first year in a helpfully explaining fashion. "BUT ALSO I AM NOT SURE WHAT SURREPTITIOUSLY ACTUALLY MEANS? IS IT SOMETHING TO DO WITH CHEESECAKE?"

"EVERYTHING IS TO DO WITH CHEESECAKE," said the first first year wisely.

Maisie turned back to Harold. "Are you all right, Mr Richardson? Because you signed that petition in a *very* purposeful fashion."

"I'm fine," said Harold.

Maisie looked at him. "Are you sure?"

There were many things that Harold could have said at this point.

But he chose the wisest of them.

"No," he said, "I don't think I've been fine for a long while. Ever since that man came to the village and the Mayor did—"

"Did what?" said Maisie. Her voice was soft and kind. "Mr Richardson, if there's something wrong, then maybe talking about it will help."

He gave her a long and suddenly very watery-eyed look. "I think that there is something very wrong and I think that maybe, I've let it happen."

"Then let's sort it out," she said. "*All* of it."

And very quietly, one of the first years handed him a biscuit.

IN WHICH, AN UNEXPECTED PHONE CALL

There is one more thing that I need to update you on and that was a phone call which was made late that night to the School of the Good Sisters. It came through to the study, just before Good Sister Christine was about to go to bed, and for a wild and wonderful moment she wondered if it were Hanna and Edie and Calla telling her that they'd found Good Sister June.

She picked it up. "Hello? Do you have her? Is she found?"

"Is that the Head of the School?" said a male voice.

Hope, thought Good Sister Christine. It came so quickly and went so fast.

She took a deep breath.

"Yes," she said. "Who is this? Can I help you?"

"Do you know what your pupils are up to? Where they all were today?"

"Yes," said Good Sister Christine. "A vast number of them were in the village carrying out geography fieldwork." She had sent Good Sister Gwendolyn and Good Sister Robin into the village to covertly keep an eye on things and help out where they could. This had involved them spending the morning in the local café and having a very nice toasted teacake at ten, and then another at eleven, and then a very very nice toasted sandwich each for lunch.

"And you let it happen? You let them *hassle* and *persecute* an innocent businessman just trying to go about his day?"

"If I believe in anything, I believe in my students doing the right thing," said Good Sister Christine. "And if the right thing involves protesting against a plan to take away the free choice of everybody to eat what they want, then I'm all in favour."

"Well, I'm in favour of good business choices," said the person.

(I think by now, you have worked out that it is William and so I shall use his name from now on.)

"And do they involve trying to take my school away from me? I know that you want the building."

"It's perfect," said William with feeling. "It's just the right size for a factory. You don't understand."

"Oh, I understand entirely," said Good Sister Christine.

"You're all the same," said William. "You think that you can control what's going on, but you can't. I run that village and everything in it now. You'll never stop me or my paste."

There was a Dramatic Pause.

Good Sister Christine did not say anything.

"I'm waiting for your reply," said William. "Don't you have anything to say to that?"

"I think that you've clearly thought a bit too much about this," said Good Sister Christine. "Have you thought about taking up a hobby? Perhaps crochet? I hear it's very calming."

William made a curious, spluttering sort of noise.

Good Sister Christine smiled. "You can do what you want and you'll never stop these girls from doing the right thing. The School of the Good Sisters isn't just about a building. It's about family—and family doesn't need a building. It just needs people who love each other very much, even when the other person is being *intensely* annoying."

There was a long pause before a sudden, vicious reply came: "I'm going to *end* your school."

"Oh, Mr Bishop, I do look forward to seeing you try," said Good Sister Christine, for she had known who it was all along.

She hung up the phone.

She took a deep breath. She counted to ten.

And then she sent Calla a text.

SOMEWHERE IN THE SEA OUTSIDE OF RUTHERFORD BAY

Calla received Good Sister Christine's message the next morning in the *Moonacre*, just as Meredith took the boat into the open sea beyond Rutherford Bay.

"Oh," she said as her phone burst into life. "I've got reception. And also a *thousand* messages. There's one from Good Sister Christine."

"Wait," said Hanna, "does she still think we've got flu?"

"No," said Calla. She looked deeply surprised. "Listen." She began to read from her phone. *"Hello, everybody. I know exactly what you're doing right now and I approve. I always have and always will approve of what you three do. Mr Bishop isn't happy with just taking over the village and making everybody eat his Kale Paste. He's trying to evict us and turn the school into a factory. He hates everything that we stand for, I think. I'll fight him for as long as I can but you need to hurry. Find Good Sister June. Bring her home. P.S. I sent you Gareth. I hope he found you. If he did, then tell him he's doing a good job and that I'm proud of him."*

Hanna looked at Gareth. "Good Sister Christine sent you? Why didn't you ever say?"

Gareth looked deeply awkward. "I wanted to but she asked me to keep it secret and she did this sort of face at me and oh, I'm so sorry—"

"It's okay. You did the right thing," said Hanna with a little smile. "Honestly, you did." She turned back to Calla. "Tell Good Sister Christine that he's doing an *amazing* job."[1]

Edie nodded. "Tell her that we are on our way to Good Sister June right now! That we will bring her back to save the school! And that I am *quite* serious about poisoning that awful man!"

Calla nodded and texted back to Good Sister Christine. And because I am a helpful author who has just had a Particularly Invigorating Pink Wafer, I am going to tell you precisely what she said:

Sorry this is a bit late. I just got reception. We're on a boat from Rutherford Bay to a place called Merlin Cove. Good Sister June was definitely there a few days ago. Hopefully she's still there now. If she is, then we might need Good Sister Paulette to get us home. I'll text you if we do. We'll be back as soon as we can. Also, Gareth is AMAZING.

Once this had sent, Calla sent another quick text to her mum[2] before putting down her phone. "I know it's

---

1 This was not a lie for that very morning, he had made a small campfire on the beach and cooked bacon and eggs for the girls and Meredith. Hanna hadn't even had to leave her nest of blankets on the boat. Gareth had brought it over and then, with a flourish, presented her with a little glass of freshly squeezed orange juice.

2 Why do ducks go to the zoo? To visit the quackodiles.

not *good* news about that man trying to take over the village and the school but it does mean that Rose is being very irritating towards him. If he's phoning Good Sister Christine directly and trying to bully her, then that means the protest is working."

"I had no doubt that it would," said Edie. "Rose is *especially* irritating, but she has also passed my Midnight Malevolency Masterclass so she does know how to lead a particularly good protest."

"And, by tomorrow, she'll have us all in person to help her as well. Good Sister June is going to be at Merlin Cove. I know it. We're going to find her and then we'll stop that kale man and we'll all be home in time for tea."

Meredith looked up from the tiller of the boat where she had been quietly steering. She looked worried. "I know that I dropped Good Sister June off at Merlin Cove but she might not be there now. Don't count your chickens before they're hatched. I don't want you to be disappointed when we get there."

"This is not about chickens," said Edie. "It is about logic. For if the dear Good Sister June needed your help to get to this cove then it is logical that she would need your assistance to get away from it. And if you were not there, then she would need the assistance of somebody else who has a boat. But if it is the first time that she has been to this place, she will not know anybody with a boat. And that all ignores the fact that if she has gone here to meet her long-lost friend and her long-lost friend is, as we suspect, here, then why would she go anywhere else at all?"

Meredith stared at Edie in a deeply impressed and slightly terrified fashion.

"It's all right," said Edie with a contented little smile. "I am French, so, I am really very good at working out this sort of thing." She returned to dangling her hand into the water. Gareth leant over and offered Meredith a sandwich. "Smoked salmon," he said, "with a small topping of dill pickle. I know you have a lot of things to process right now and a sandwich will help with that. Trust me."

Calla bumped Hanna with her elbow. "Those two are *so* going to get married."

When Hanna did not immediately reply, Calla did not say anything. She simply sat back and waited for when, and indeed if, her friend would tell her what was wrong.

And because they were best friends, Hanna did.

"Did I ever tell you about why I read so much?" she said.

"No," said Calla.

"I read because it makes me feel less by myself," said Hanna. "You have your mum and Edie has her parents but I don't have anything like that. I never have. All I had was Good Sister June. My parents are like strangers to me. We talk and send letters and things to each other but I don't know them. Not properly. But the things I read—I *know* them. I always have. They've always made sense to me. Whenever I've been worried or thinking about something too much and haven't known what to do, Good Sister June and the books we read together

258

helped me out. They showed me what to do and how to do it."

Calla looked sad. "You're talking like this is all in the past. Showed. Helped."

"Because it is," said Hanna. "Because I don't know what to do. I've been trying to work it out all along, I think. Ever since we left the school. I've been guided by stories. The books I've read and the story of the notebook. The story of Good Sister June and me. The story of the three of us. And I've always known what to do because of everything I've ever read. But I think—maybe—I don't have anything to help me with this bit. I don't know how this is going to end."

"Maybe all you have to do is keep going," said Calla wisely. "And we'll figure out the ending when we get there. Together."

MERLIN COVE

After about twenty minutes on the open sea, Meredith turned the *Moonacre* towards the cliffs. When they got so close that they could almost touch it and the waves started to crash and whirl all around them, Calla rolled purposefully into the middle of the boat and climbed underneath Gareth's bench to hide. She was joined there by Edie, who was muttering something very heartfelt in French,[1] and Hanna would have joined them but she couldn't take her eyes off what was happening. She felt as if they were moments from sinking but somehow, she had never felt more alive.

Hanna looked over at Meredith. Her eyes were bright and she had braced herself against the side of the boat, leaning into the waves and the water as it tossed the *Moonacre* all around. When an enormous wave came that splashed the entire boat, Meredith greeted it with a smile and a wild laugh.

"Almost there!" she said, when she noticed that Hanna was watching her. "That's where we're going!" She gestured

---

1 "*Oh, comme je voudrais un macaron en ce moment*" which roughly translates into "Oh, how I would like a macaron right now".

at a gap in the cliff. It was barely even the width of the boat and framed by dark, wet rocks, wrapped in seaweed. It was almost completely invisible from even a few metres away.

Meredith looked as if she was part sea-creature, thought Hanna. She was completely at home on the water and the way she handled the boat. She was like something out of— And then all of a sudden, Hanna found herself struggling for references. Meredith wasn't like something out of a book or a myth or a legend. She was herself and that was what mattered. And by the look on Gareth's face, he clearly thought that as well. He hadn't taken his eyes off her.

The *Moonacre* suddenly jerked to the right and then almost spun in a complete circle. She[1] was caught in a chaotic eddy of water and the moment that the waves seemed to take her, Meredith crouched down and gunned the motor. The boat roared forward and into another twist of water, pulling to the left and then the right as though she was dancing with somebody but didn't know the steps. Hanna gripped her bench so tightly that her knuckles grew white.

Gareth locked his eyes on Meredith. He said, "Meredith—?"

Meredith glanced over at him. "Trust me," she said, with a wild smile.[2]

---

1 Boats are always a "she".
2 Gareth, faintly: "I think I love you."

But then Meredith slammed the *Moonacre* into another sharp turn. Hanna grabbed the side as the boat bounced over another wave before sliding through the gap in the cliffs as if she had been doing it all her life. The water turned quiet and still. Hanna opened her eyes. In the distance was a deserted, golden beach and beyond that, a cottage.

Meredith pointed the *Moonacre* towards it.

A QUICK NOTE FROM
YOUR NARRATOR

And now, I must tell you something that I have been trying to tell you about for a very long time.

I have tried to tell you this before and I have got it wrong, so many times.

But then, at last, I realized what I had to do.

I just had to tell you what happened.

Just the facts.

Even when it hurt.

Even then.

THE DAY IT ALL BEGAN

Several weeks earlier, Good Sister June had woken up at three a.m. It was not a choice of hers to wake at three a.m. but rather something she had done every night for the past few months. All of a sudden, her mind leapt into action and then, even though her eyes and body did not want to admit it, she would be wide awake and wondering what to do with herself. Some nights, she would lie there and stubbornly will herself back to sleep, but on other nights, when this did not work, she would walk the halls of the School of the Good Sisters and wonder what on earth was happening to her and why she could no longer sleep.[1]

And the more that Good Sister June did not sleep, the more that she began to fade from the world. She began to lose track of time and would find herself forgetting to do things or not even remembering what they were in the first place. She would be late for breakfast and early for lunch and sometimes, during the day, when the rooms were warm and the other sisters had left her by

1 I do not know if you have ever experienced something similar, but it changes you when you do not sleep. You become fainter, somehow, as if you are not quite fully in the world. Like a drawing that hasn't been filled in yet, or a song that has not yet been sung.

herself for a few moments, she found her eyes closing as she slowly fell asleep. She never slept for long enough though. It would just be for moments and then she would wake and feel more tired than she had even before she'd closed her eyes.

On the nights when it all grew too much to bear, Good Sister June got out of her bed and headed towards the library to distract herself with books. Books did not ask her questions about the life she had led or the losses she had known. They simply let her forget everything for a short while and that was enough. She would sit in her favourite armchair and read. She read her way through myths and fairy tales and adventures, and she read them so late at night and so early in the morning that the world would almost stop around her.

A part of her wondered what she would do when the girls came back, but a greater part of her, the part that ached with exhaustion, simply wanted to sleep. Nothing more. Nothing less. Just to sleep and to rest.

One morning when she was so tired that she wasn't even sure what day it was any more, Good Sister June had found herself looking through the newspapers in the library. It was not something that she usually did and she was not sure why she was doing it.

And if she had not done it that day, then this story would not have even been a story at all.

But it is a story because she turned the first few pages of that newspaper over and then, all of a sudden, came across a short article about a bakery.

WHAT THE NEWSPAPER SAID

Next to the article was a picture of the bakery. The sign was old and faded but it was still there.

Bishop & Family

Good Sister June could not take her eyes off it. All of the memories that she had spent so long trying to forget had not been forgotten at all. They were as fresh and sharp and as painful as they were the day that they had been made. She remembered it all. The way that the shop had looked when she'd walked up to it on that last, fateful day. The way that its emptiness had broken her heart. The way that they had left her, all alone.

"Lily," she said. "Georgia. Sarah."

Their names. They still felt right to her. She hadn't said them for years. And yet here they were, still inside her heart. She'd spent so long running away from the hurtful memories of her time with Lily and Georgia and Sarah that she had forgotten about what they had actually meant to her. They had been precious and painful but *good*.

She stood up then and went over to where the notebook was on the shelf. After all of these years, she still remembered exactly where it was. She brought it back down to the table and began to flick through it. Her hands shook with every page that she turned. She could almost *hear* Lily and Georgia and Sarah. All of it was still there. All of their friendship. The memories.

When she reached the final page of the notebook, she glanced back at the article. There was no mention of Sarah or Georgia but it did say that Lily was ill. She was near death. But that meant that she was still alive.

And that meant that she could find her.

Her best friend might still be out there.

Good Sister June stood up and went to her study. She took the small amount of money that she had and put it in a pocket, deep inside her habit.[1] In her other pocket she placed a handful of biscuits. She picked up a pen and wrote the note for Good Sister Christine and left it for her to discover before she walked out of the room.

And then she took one step forward and then another until she was closing the front door behind her and walking down the long lane into the village and by the time Good Sister Christine had realized that she was missing, Good Sister June was already gone.

---

1 This is a fancy word for the sort of dress that nuns wear.

SPUN SUGAR COTTAGE

Good Sister June did not know what she was looking for but she knew that it had to start with a bakery. She began by visiting all of the ones in the local villages, and then she went to all of the ones in the towns beyond that. She took buses to Malton and to Pickering before getting a train up to Cayton and then on to Filey and Scarborough, and all of the towns that lay beyond.

One day, she came across a bakery in Whitby which sold a candyfloss cake.

And then she had followed the crumbs all the way to Merlin Cove.

Where there was a small path up from the beach to the cottage. Good Sister June followed it past a boat piled high with tarpaulins and boxes and wondered, for the first time, if Lily had got married. The man in the article had been a great-nephew. Perhaps Lily had had children of her own as well. Perhaps they were there now at the cottage with her and asking why a woman dressed a little bit like a penguin was walking up from the beach to see them.

At the end of the path was a fence, a gate and a small

sign that said *Spun Sugar Cottage*. Underneath this, somebody had written another word: *Welcome*.

Good Sister June took a step forward and then pushed the gate open and stepped through the hedge. It revealed a long and slender patch of garden, the width of two people at its widest, and at the end of it was a tiny cottage that was almost completely white save for a red front door and bright yellow flowers that had been planted in boxes in front of every window.

A part of Good Sister June felt hot and another part of her felt cold, and there was a third part, somewhere down inside her stomach, which felt absolutely nothing at all.

She took a deep breath and counted to ten.

Oh be brave, she thought, *be brave*.

She took a step forward and then, moving more on instinct than anything else, took another step and then another until she was right in front of the door.

She rang the doorbell.

It was answered by a woman. She was pale and slender and wore her long hair in plaits. Her eyes were the colour of the sea. She said, "Hello?" and then, "Oh! You're a nun." One of her long plaits slid forward over her shoulder. "I've seen them before—on the television, I mean—but never in real life. Wow. We don't get visitors here and then, all of a sudden, I get a nun. Wow. Okay. Can I help you?"

"I hope so," said Good Sister June. "I'm looking for Lily Bishop. I think she lives here. I mean, I hope that—she does."

The woman took a step back.

"She does," she said. "I mean, she did. I mean—I'm so—so sorry. She died. Two days ago. In her sleep. I'm so sorry. You didn't know?"

"No," said Good Sister June. "I didn't."

TO LIVE WELL IS DIVINE

There were many things that Good Sister June could have done at that point and she chose the first which came to mind.

Which was to faint, quite completely, on the doorstep.

When she awoke, she was lying in a bed in the middle of a room. It was full of light and somebody had tucked a patchwork blanket in around her. One window in the room was open and, in the distance, she could hear the sound of waves. Her habit had been placed on a chair in the corner of the room and next to it was a plate full of sandwiches which had had the crusts cut off. And it was this detail, more than anything else, which told Good Sister June that she was somewhere safe.

She got out of bed slowly and began to wrap her coif[1] back around her head. The material had been washed and all of the starch and salt of the seaside air had gone. As she carefully tucked her hair inside it and got dressed, Good Sister June felt as if she was putting it all on for the first time. It was as if she was still

---

1 This is a fancy word for the white scarf that nuns wrap around their hair.

the girl who had gone to Good Sister Gladys all those years ago.

Maybe she was still that girl, she thought. Maybe growing up wasn't about leaving the person who you were behind but learning how to take her with you.

Suddenly there was a gentle knock at the door and it was pushed open. "Hello? I heard movement and I wondered if you were awake?" It was the same woman that had answered the door.

"Yes," said Good Sister June. "Where am I?"

She must have been asleep for at least a day, she thought, or maybe more. The woman was wearing her hair differently and had changed her clothes.

"You're still in the cottage," said the woman. "We decided not to move you."

Good Sister June sat down on the edge of the bed. "We?"

"The doctor. I called him the moment you fainted. As soon as I said that there was a nun on my doorstep and told him everything, he was right over.[1] He helped me get you into the bed and said to just let you sleep. Exhaustion, he said."

"Thank you," said Good Sister June. "I've not been sleeping well for a long while now. And then, I think, the news was such a shock."

1 The doctor's name was Mr Irons and he is almost as good as Good Sister Paulette in helicopter flying. Although not *as* good. Now that they have made friends, they are very fond of having races and I am delighted to say that Good Sister Paulette beats him every time.

"I'm sorry," said the woman.

"It's okay," said Good Sister June.

"You'll be wanting to know my name," said the woman.

"Yes," said Good Sister June, because she was.

"I'm Jessie," said Jessie. "Jessie Palmer. I am—was—Miss Bishop's live-in help. I've been sorting things out. All of the admin, you know."

"My name is Good Sister June," said Good Sister June.

A curious look of interest passed over Jessie's face. "Do you have a surname at all?"

"No," said Good Sister June. "It's just Good Sister June. The whole thing, all at once, and then that's it. No more and no less. It's one of the rules of my order."

Jessie nodded. "Okay," she said. She picked up the plate full of sandwiches and handed them over to Good Sister June. "Eat one before you go any further, please, Good Sister June. And then I'm sure you have lots more questions to ask me. I'll answer all that I can."

Good Sister June ate the sandwich slowly. She had questions. Thousands of them. She wanted to know about Sarah and then Georgia and about how the sisters had lived their lives and where they had been and what had brought Lily back to live so near to Little Hampden but leave the bakery lost and abandoned. She wanted to know how Lily had died, the detail of it seemed suddenly important, the hope that she had not suffered, the hope that she had just closed her eyes in this postcard cottage and that she had died a simple and lovely death.

But then Good Sister June found herself asking a question that she did not expect.

"Did she live well?"

And because this question might not make sense to you, I shall explain it a little bit.

Good Sister June was asking if Lily had been given cake for her birthday rather than having to buy it herself; if she had been able to eat chips down on the beach front and watch the sun slowly set; if this cottage, so clean and bright, had been all that she had ever wanted it to be; and if she had gone on from Little Hampden and explored the world and had a job that made her happy and been able to live, in a way that did not make her scared when the bills came in.

But most of all, she was asking if Lily had been loved.

And this is what Jessie said:

"Lily—Miss Bishop—would let people stay here. Anybody who needed help or didn't have anywhere else to go—she welcomed them in. And they were so grateful but so shy, so nervous. I would be here working and I'd see them going round the house like ghosts. But she'd bring them out of themselves. She'd get them in the kitchen and cooking with her and just like that, they'd open back up again. They'd cook us things and share it with us and even when they moved on, they'd send back gifts and presents for her. At Christmas, they'd all invite her round and we'd go from home to home like we were the most important people on the face of the planet."

Which was a long and very adult way of saying:
Yes, Lily had been loved.
She had been loved so very much.

NIGHT AND DAY

There were other questions that Good Sister June had, of course, and Jessie answered all of them. She told her about how the three sisters had had to leave Little Hampden so quickly when Sarah got ill: "There was only one surgeon who could treat her and he lived at the other end of the country." And then about how the operation had failed and Sarah had died.

She told Good Sister June about how Lily and Georgia hadn't been able to open up the bakery again. There were too many memories in it. She told her about how, instead, the sisters had hopped from village to village along the coast, never settling in one place for long until one day they found Merlin Cove and never left. Somewhere along the way, Georgia had become interested in family history.

"She got them to put her father's name on the memorial in Filey, you know, for the war dead," said Jessie thoughtfully. "And then she discovered a great-nephew that they never knew they had."

Jessie had pulled a face when she got to this point. "I've never liked the boy if I'm honest. The Miss Bishops were amazing at baking. That's how they earned some money—teaching people and selling what they made.

But this nephew of theirs, he made them stop. Said that food that wasn't made out of kale wasn't worth having. He even wanted that bakery of theirs in Little Hampden so he could use it for his own plans. Lily gave him the key to shut him up but she didn't officially give him the property. Wouldn't do that however much he badgered her. And he did. It wasn't nice. He's not a good man."

And then, at last, Jessie told her that Georgia had died. "It was only a year ago and it was a good death. I think she was ready for it. She had finished all of her library books." It was the sort of detail that made Good Sister June have a Tiny Cry and then Jessie had one as well and they both had to distract themselves by making afternoon tea in a heartfelt and Let's Stop Crying And Have A Bun sort of manner.[1]

That evening, Good Sister June began to feel suddenly awkward. "I can go," she said, "You don't need somebody like me to worry about right now. You already have enough to deal with."

Jessie had refused. Instead she had asked Good Sister June to stay the night and then the night after that so that she could go to Lily's funeral and, suddenly too tired to argue, Good Sister June had agreed to do so. She slept in the same room as before and left the windows open throughout the night and woke up with the dawn. By the time Jessie was awake, Good Sister June was halfway through making croissants for breakfast and

1 Which is a very British talent indeed.

already had a Victoria sponge baking in the oven for that afternoon.

"I haven't baked for years," she said as Jessie sat down at the kitchen table. "I stopped all of a sudden and then I never started again."

And when she was washing up their empty plates, Good Sister June realized that she had slept the whole night through.

THE READING SKILLS OF SAMUEL WEISENREIDER

The funeral for Lily Bishop was held on a warm and perfect day and when it was all over and Good Sister June was wondering if she could cry any more, Jessie asked her to come to the solicitor's with her.

"It's the last thing I need to do today," said Jessie. "He needs to tell me about the will and what to do with Miss Bishop's house. I'd like it if you were there."[1]

The solicitor's name was Mr Weisenreider and his office was tucked into the corner of a busy street in Whitby. "My cousin twice removed knew one of the sisters when she was young,"[2] he said, as he welcomed them in. "We got back in touch when Miss Bishop—Georgia—was researching her family history. I've acted for them ever

[1] A "will" is a fancy word for a document that tells people what to do with somebody's things when that somebody dies. Wills are really just a list of instructions about the things that somebody loves very much and wants to make sure that they are looked after. For example, my will includes instructions about my collection of cake display stands and also, all of the books in the library at school.

[2] This means that they were his grandmother's cousin. Every generation means a "removed". It is all very complicated, I know, so let's nod in a knowing fashion, have a custard cream and move on.

since.[1] There's a lot to sort out. The cottage and the bakery, for example. I understand that the latter is being run by young Mr Bishop at the moment?"

Jessie scowled. "Not officially. He just turned up one day and browbeat her into giving him the key. Wouldn't shut up until she did. The arrogance of him. I thought he was there to tell her how sorry he was about her diagnosis but no, just after the bakery. She wasn't even dead."

"Ideally he'd have been here today. I've left his office a number of messages and I even called in there before the funeral, but no response." Mr Weisenreider gestured into the room. "In here, please. Do take a seat."

"I'm not surprised. I've never trusted him."

"Be that as it may, Miss Bishop had some very specific wishes about the properties when she died. It's a shame that he's not here for the reading of them," said Mr Weisenreider. He began to rummage through the papers on the desk. "I'm sure I've got the file here. Ah yes. Here it is. Okay. Before I tell you about the property, I have to do something else. It's quite unusual but Miss Bishop—she was rather a character. I really did have a lot of time for her. I shall miss our chats." He produced an envelope and gave Good Sister June and Jessie a smile.

"Let's begin," he said. "Miss Bishop asked that I begin the proceedings by giving this letter to a certain individual.

1 This does not mean that Mr Weisenreider had performed a play for the Bishop sisters but rather that he had looked after their legal affairs and written Strongly Worded Letters.

She was not sure if that person would be here and so, if they weren't, I was to dispose of the letter without reading it. But the person *is* here and so it's time to hand it over."

Good Sister June looked at Jessie. "It's for you," she said. "Oh, I'm so glad."

Jessie looked at Good Sister June. A slow smile crossed her face. "Look at the envelope."

And so Good Sister June did and she realized that the envelope was not for Jessie.

It was for her.

DEAREST JUNE

Dearest June,

I hope you get this. I'm so sorry that I can't be there with you when—if—you do.

I think about you a lot. I try to work out how you might have changed over the years. If you still look like the girl that I remember or if you've changed at all. I don't think you will have. I think you'll be just the same.

Georgia tells me that she could hire a detective to try and find you but I've always stopped her. I'm not sure why. Guilt, I think. Fear, maybe. We were such good friends and we just left you without a word. I don't know what I'd do if I found you and you didn't want to see me. Perhaps it's better like this. I don't know. I just know that I've missed you all my life.

We left breadcrumbs for you in the hope that you'd find them and then us. We taught people how to make the recipes that we'd talked about all those years ago. Candyfloss cake. Do you remember? And Victoria sponge, everywhere. We also lived in the places that we'd planned for the café. We hoped that somehow you would find us.

The biggest breadcrumb was the bakery. We never sold it. We hoped that maybe one day you'd come back to it, but I knew you wouldn't. We just disappeared. I wouldn't have been able to even look at the bakery if I were you. It would have hurt too much.

Oh, June, I hope you've lived a perfect life. I hope you know your family never forgot you. I hope you know that you were never alone.

I hope you know how much we loved you, all along.

All my love,

Your sister, Lily

HOPE AFTER READING

Good Sister June sat there for a long time after reading that letter. It was only when Mr Weisenreider coughed and offered her a tissue that she realized that she was crying as well.

"It's all right," said Mr Weisenreider in a gentle and tactful fashion. "Grief is a wave. It comes and it goes. You mustn't fight it. That's the secret. Never fight it." He turned back to his papers. "We have a lot left to cover. Are you all right if I continue?"

Good Sister June nodded. "Yes," she said softly. "Of course."

And so Mr Weisenreider continued. Lily had wanted her money to go to local charities and some of her books to be given to those who had never had a book of their own. There were other things to be decided and discussed but Good Sister June only heard half of it. She had the most precious thing of all in her letter. She would never let it go. Even now, she could not bear to put it in her pocket. She kept unfolding it and rereading it.

But then, when Mr Weisenreider mentioned the cottage at Merlin Cove, she found herself suddenly paying attention.

"Miss Bishop left it to you, Jessie, to do with as you will. The only rule is that you cannot sell it. It has to stay within the family, so to speak."

Family was not just about who you were related to, thought Good Sister June suddenly. It was about who remembered you at the end. She squeezed Jessie's hand. "I'm thrilled for you," she said. "It's your home now, forever. I can't imagine anything more perfect."

"And then there's the bakery," said Mr Weisenreider. He paused and studied the two women thoughtfully. "I am aware that Mr Bishop is currently in charge of the property but Miss Bishop allowed this only as a very temporary state of affairs. He's fully aware that he might have to give the property up but, as he informed me when we last spoke, he does not see this happening. I was not able to tell him then what I am about to tell you now. Client confidentiality forbade me. Miss Bishop made a decision about the bakery and it was a... conditional one. There were certain things that had to happen beforehand and if they didn't, then the bakery would go to Mr Bishop. But those things have happened. One of those things is sitting before me, right now. And so I am able to follow Miss Bishop's wishes just as she wanted."

Time stood still for a moment. A seagull wheeled past the window. In the distance, people paddled in the sea.

And then he said it: "Miss Bishop has left the bakery to you, Good Sister June. Lily wanted it to go to you. It's yours. The bakery, it's yours."

NO WOMAN IS AN ISLAND

And so, at last, we come to Rutherford Bay, just in time to see a boat arriving at the sand as though it was always meant to be there. Two of the passengers get out and pull it up onto the beach and then the other three get out. They talk for a moment amongst themselves before one girl steps forward. She carries a notebook which is full of the dreams of three other hopeful young girls. She holds it like treasure.

She walks along the beach towards the cottage. She walks past the sign for *Spun Sugar Cottage* and trails her fingers over the top of the tallest flowers in the garden. And when she reaches the front door, she knocks twice and takes a brief, suddenly nervous step back. She makes herself stop from taking another. Instead, she inhales and thinks about her friends and the way that they believed in this quest, right from the start.

The door is opened by a woman who is tall and slender and dressed a little bit like a penguin. Her eyes grow wide. She does not speak.

The girl holds out the notebook to her.

The woman takes it.

And then the other person in the house, a woman with hair the colour of twilight, comes to the door. She looks at the girl and then back at the woman who looks a little bit like a penguin. She raises her eyebrows in a question.

The woman who looks a little bit like a penguin speaks. Her voice is quiet, raw. "This is Hanna," she says, "and those people beyond her, that's Calla and Edie and Gareth."

There is a long pause.

And then she says, "They're my family."

STARTING OVER

That night, Merlin Cove hosted a party like it had never seen. Gareth built a campfire on the beach which was twice the height of Spun Sugar Cottage and they roasted chicken and corn on the cobs in the glowing heart of the fire and had enormous marshmallows for afters. It was the sort of meal that felt like it might never end. Everybody kept talking and whenever somebody paused, another person would remember something and they would burst into laughter and start all over again. When it got cold, Meredith handed out blankets from the *Moonacre* for everybody to wrap themselves up in, and when it grew dark, Gareth headed up to Spun Sugar Cottage with Jessie to arrange cushions and rugs in the front room for everybody to sleep on. They brought back with them thermoses full of hot chocolate and when Gareth sat back down to drink his, he accidentally on purpose sat next to Meredith and Hanna was sure that she saw hearts in his eyes.

And when all the stories were told, and all of the jokes had been made, Calla gave Edie a meaningful look. It was the sort of look that said, "I think Good Sister June and Hanna might need a private moment." Edie nodded and gave her a look back which said, "I think that as well so let's go to bed and let them have it. Also, do you think Jessie might have some macarons tucked away somewhere?"

The two of them stood up, wished everybody goodnight, and headed back up to the cottage. They were swiftly followed by Meredith and Jessie, the two of them walking up to the cottage with their arms around each other like the oldest and best of friends. Gareth stood up a short while after that. He paused only to give Good Sister June a fierce and heartfelt hug before he left.

And then it was just Good Sister June and Hanna at the campfire, looking at each other as though they were seeing each other for the very first time.

"I'm sorry," said Good Sister June eventually. "I should have shared with you what had happened. I shouldn't have just disappeared. Running away never solves anything."

Hanna studied the nun in a thoughtful fashion. "It's okay," she said.

"No," said Good Sister June, who was determined to have Heartfelt Adult Guilt over the entire situation. "I'm meant to be your Headmistress. I have responsibilities and I just left them behind."

Hanna shrugged. "It's okay," she said again.

"You don't have to say that. I just keep thinking about what I put you through and how it must have felt. That moment when I should have been there for you and I wasn't. All the things that you thought might have happened to me. And now the school's under threat? It's all my fault. I should have been there to stop that dreadful man. All of it. I shouldn't have just run away from it all—"

Hanna held up her hand. "Hang on."

Good Sister June waited for her to say something else but she didn't. Instead Hanna rummaged in her bag and took out a book. It was her copy of *Eustacia Goes to the Chalet School*. She handed it over to Good Sister June.

"Read me some," she said, "please. From the beginning. Would you?"

Good Sister June took a deep breath. She rubbed her eyes.

And then she began.

A QUICK WORD FROM YOUR NARRATOR

That is one ending but there is another yet to come. And in the next chapter, I shall tell you all about it.

THE SECOND ENDING

William Bishop had not slept well after the Incident at the bakery. He kept dreaming about dangling girls appearing out of nowhere before him and disappearing, just as he was about to go and do a Heartfelt Yell at them. And when he was not dreaming about Heartfelt Yelling, he was dreaming about the nuns from that awful school lining up outside of the bakery and pelting him with exquisitely iced cupcakes. It was horrendous.

When he woke up, he made a series of increasingly grumpy phone calls. The first was to Stuart Simpson at the police station where he told him, "If you don't arrest every single one of those girls the moment that they arrive at the bakery, then I'll have you arrested instead." The second was to the governors at the School of the Good Sisters to request a meeting that "would be a most... profitable... endeavour"[1] and the third was to Dominic Burton to request that within the next six months Little Hampden would pass a law to ban girls

---

[1] The little dots here indicate the moments during the phone call where William paused for Dramatic Effect. They do not indicate me falling asleep on the keyboard.

under the age of thirteen years old and replace them with courgettes.

All of this Purposeful Meanness made William feel a lot better. He celebrated by having a kale smoothie for breakfast and heading off towards the bakery ready to continue his plans for the redecoration. As he unlocked the front door to the shop, he heard a helicopter pass overhead. He paused only briefly to look up before stepping inside. A part of him wondered how long it might take before the bakery properly became his. He had not heard from his great-aunt for a long while but he was not particularly worried about that. He had spent so long by himself that he was rather used to the loneliness.

There was a sudden knock on the door.

William swung around. His whole body was ready to yell. It was one of the girls, he thought, they'd come back.

But it was Stuart instead. He pushed open the door and came inside. "I thought you promised me people to arrest?" He gestured outside. "There's nothing here but pigeons."

"They'll come," said William. "I know it."

"Well, I can't stay here forever. I have a job to do."

"You'll stay here however long I want you to stay."

Stuart took a deep breath. He counted to ten. He was starting to think that he had made the wrong choice in taking the bribes from William. He really was very bossy.

All of a sudden, William froze. He stared into the distance. "Do you hear that?"

"Do I hear *what*?" said Stuart.

"That."

Stuart looked concerned. "There's nothing there. You're imagining things."

"No," said William. He took a deep breath. "I'm not."

Because the enormous group of people marching towards the bakery, was so very, very real.

YOU'VE GOT TO FIGHT FOR YOUR RIGHT TO PROTEST

Rose Bastable was having the time of her life. On one side of her, she had Lucy Millais and on the other, Maisie Holloway, and behind them were Eloise Taylor, Sethi and Sabia Gopal; Ellen Beaufort; Lily Maguire; Sally Campbell; Jia Liu and a great and glorious crowd of girls ranging from first years to the very tall and almost adult girls in their final year.

And behind this remarkable line-up were more people still. Good Sister Christine was walking alongside Good Sister Gwendolyn and Good Sister Robin, and even Good Sister Honey had left her beloved kitchen behind for the day. The whole school was marching on the bakery and they were not alone.

All of their old friends had joined them and all of their new friends as well. Harold Richardson had put in a traffic diversion overnight so that they could march without interruption, before then joining a group of first years and giving them an impromptu lecture on Expressing Your Basic Human Right To Protest.

With every step, the crowd had grown bigger. As they headed past the retirement home, the residents rose from their seats and came out to join them. They were led by a woman called Lisette Bertolini, a silvery-haired and tiny warrior, who was promptly adopted by a crowd of first years who tucked their arms in with hers. They listened adoringly to the stories of her brave and fearless great-grandmother and how she had come to Little Hampden as a refugee many years ago[1] and then to the tales of the other retirees who brought with them placards and rainbow-coloured flags and spoke about their own protests at places like Greenham Common and Stonewall.

Just before they'd arrived at the bakery, the girls marched past Little Hampden village hall where the parent and toddler group were busy singing songs. All of the colour and noise caught the eye of the group leader, a woman called Mila Van Dam, and then when she saw what they were protesting about and thought of her own great-grandmother[2] and the way that she had spent her life thinking of others, Mila led the toddlers and parents out to join them. Several toddlers, whose legs were just that little bit too small to cope with the march, were immediately hoisted onto the shoulders of the tallest girls, whilst the others were swung up in the arms of the first years, and their parents given restorative jammie dodgers and told that they were doing a Very Good Job by Good Sister Honey and her band of benevolent biscuit-toting assistants.

---

1 Who you have met elsewhere in this book.
2 Who you have also met elsewhere in this book.

"I think they're coming here," said Stuart, once he had taken all of this in.

William turned on him, furious. "Then why on earth aren't you stopping them?"

Stuart did not reply. This was not because he did not have anything to say but rather that his police radio had suddenly fizzed into life. And even though he did not wish to admit it, or even really knew it himself these days, underneath all of Stuart's bad choices and bribe-taking still lay the good policeman that he always wanted to be and good policemen answered their radio. He pulled his radio out of his pocket. "Is there somebody on this channel? Repeat yourself if you are. I didn't hear your last transmission."

"It's me, Stuart, it's Harold," said Harold Richardson. "I know we've not been best friends but please, you have to listen to me. I bet that man is trying to get you to arrest everybody right now. You don't have to do that. You know that they're just practising their democratic right to protest. You can't do anything unless they use or threaten somebody or something with violence. You know that. So make a choice."

The radio cut out.

Stuart glanced over at William. "He's right," he said. He realized that he was suddenly very relieved. "I can't do anything about a march. They're perfectly within their rights to do this. Legally, I have to let it happen."

"Oh, I'll show you legalities," said William. He pressed his knuckles to his forehead and took a deep breath. Even though the march was making a lot of noise, he could hear the curious slapping sound of a helicopter's rotor blade underneath it all. This was starting to prove very stressful. He needed a way to make it end.

And then he realized that he had a way.

He picked up his phone and made a call. "Get here. I don't care if you're seen. Now. I need you. NOW. It's time for you to pay me back."

Rose's march was now only two storefronts away. With every step the girls took, William saw and heard something new. One of the nuns was busily teaching the girls, and indeed anybody who would listen, about how to camouflage yourself inside a crowd[1] whilst another nun, with the aid of several first years, was handing out boxes full of freshly made cannoli to the marchers from the retirement home. Another nun had even broken into song and although the words were not particularly clear, nor was the tune especially tuneful, there was something deeply thrilling about the way she sang it. It was almost as if she was leading the girls into battle.

For a moment, William thought that the girls might march all the way into the bakery. He began to think wildly about escape routes and how far he might be able to run through the crowd before they stopped him, but then the march came to a gentle halt just short of the

---

1 The secret is to look normal and like you're meant to be there. People notice the unusual things and so they will see the person who is trying to hide rather than the person who is not.

bakery. Rose lifted up her right hand in a pre-arranged signal and chairs began to appear from nowhere for the elder members of the protest to have a nice sit down. From somewhere else came freshly iced buns, some studded with sharp bites of crystallized ginger and others swelling with custardy insides, and from somewhere else came the soft sound of an impromptu story time being held for the tiniest members of the protest and anybody else who cared to listen.

And if William had been paying especial attention to what else was happening, he would have noticed that some of the other first years were wearing high visibility vests and clearing a big space in the middle of the park opposite the bakery, and he would have also noticed that the noise of the helicopter which had been hanging around all morning was suddenly back and louder than before, but he didn't because he wasn't paying attention at all.

And Rose Bastable was very happy about that.

"Hello, Mr Bishop," said Rose.

She gave him a contented smile before an unexpected noise caught her attention. Suddenly concerned, she turned around to see a grown man pushing his way through the crowd towards her. His face was red and he was sweating and he looked very much as if he did not want to be there at all.

The first years did not quite know what to do with him. They glanced at Rose. She gestured at them to allow him through. When he was within earshot, she said, "Hello! You're the new Mayor of Little Hampden, aren't you? We were coming to see you later today. We've got a petition to give you against the kale café plans. Nobody wants it."

The noise of the helicopter grew even louder.

Dominic Burton thought longingly of the new and terribly expensive watch he had on order. "I don't want to see your petition. It's time for you all to go home. I've just passed a bylaw that says gatherings like this are illegal."

"I thought it took thirty days for bylaws to become legal."[1]

"Well, I signed it thirty days ago," said Dominic. "It's time for this protest to go home."

"Oh no," said Rose with a smile. "We're not a protest. We're a distraction."

And it was then that William noticed the helicopter coming in to land.

[1] Knowing this sort of thing is one of the Extraordinary Skills of the pupils of the School of the Good Sisters and I am so proud of them.

THE BEGINNING OF THE END

Several people got out of the helicopter. There were three girls,[1] two women, two men, and then a very small and penguin-like nun. When the first years saw this individual, they burst into rapturous cheers. Several of the more emotional of them fainted from over-excitement and had to be brought back to life with bourbon creams, carefully wafted under their nostrils, whilst several others began to do an impromptu dance of joy which slowly spread around the whole crowd until everybody was dancing and waving their banners, and in the middle of all this commotion, the nun who had got out of the helicopter stood and wondered how she could have ever let any of this go.

But then she took a deep breath and walked over to where William was standing. She brought with her one of the men who had got off the helicopter and as they got closer, William suddenly recognized him as his great-aunt's solicitor. Here. Now. And that meant only one thing.

[1] One of which said, "THE ENEMY, AT LAST I SEE HIM, LET ME CLONK HIM ON THE HEAD WITH A MACARON," and had to be Tactfully Persuaded that now was not the moment for macaron clonking by her two best friends in the entire world.

"Hello, Mr Bishop," said Mr Weisenreider, for it was he. "You're quite a difficult man to get hold of. We've been leaving you messages for the past few days."

"She's dead," said William. He felt as if he was in somebody else's body. This wasn't happening. None of it was meant to be like this.

Mr Weisenreider nodded. "Yes," he said. "I've been handling her will and estate."

William stared at him. "Did she leave me the bakery?"

"No," said Mr Weisenreider. "It's time for you to hand over the keys."

"No," said William.

And it was then that several unfortunate things happened all at once.

SEVERAL VERY
UNFORTUNATE THINGS
HAPPENING ALL AT ONCE

William's "No" coincided with Good Sister Robin pausing for breath in her song and so she overheard everything. It appalled her so much that she let out a squeak of horror which was then misinterpreted by the nearest first years as the next line of the song and something which they should repeat. The result was a cacophonous sound, the likes of which had never been heard in Little Hampden before, and which made many of the nearest toddlers burst into tears and William say rude things[1] and gesture angrily at them to stop.

The only problem was that this gesture was misinterpreted by several of the other first years, who were serving rejuvenating snacks to Lisette Bertolini and her fellow retirees, as a request by William to try some of their baked goods. Deeply excited at this change in his behaviour, they promptly began to advance upon William with trays full of cake pops and caramel slices and tiny, exquisitely iced fondant fancies. The only issue was that

---

[1] "SPIRULINA SMOOTHIES!"

the trays were so full that the carriers did not see the crack in the paving stones ahead of them.

And because Dominic Burton had not been spending the council money on fixing the paving stones of Little Hampden and had instead been increasingly spending it on himself, the first years who walked over the cracks in the paving stones ended up doing some rather spectacular somersaults which resulted in the contents of their trays flying straight towards William Bishop and the small group of people who surrounded him.

It was at this point that Gareth, who had watched all of this happen, made his move. He launched himself forward and somersaulted over the toddlers who were now being cuddled and comforted, and headed straight towards Mr Weisenreider and Good Sister June where, without stopping, he gathered Mr Weisenreider under one arm and Good Sister June under the other and bore them both to safety.

This meant that the only people left for the baked goods to land upon were Dominic Burton and William Bishop. Dominic received a cream puff to the forehead, several chocolate chip muffins to his stomach, and several doughnut holes landed neatly inside his ears. It was at this point that he rather breathlessly realized that all of this had been witnessed by people who had votes in the next election and so he tried to leave. The only problem was that Maisie Holloway and Harold Richardson were in his way.

"Hello, Mr Mayor," said Mr Richardson. "It's a funny thing. It turns out that when an elected official like yourself threatens young girls and turns out to have been taking bribes, not a lot of people like that. It's time for you to be arrested."

"I bet you wish you'd looked at our petition now," said Maisie.

And then, of course, there was William himself. At the precise moment Dominic had been hit by the cake, William had taken a step back and thought that it might miss him. It did not.

An iced bun hit his forehead and then slid stickily down his face, leaving a trail of raspberry jam and icing sugar behind it. Several doughnuts bounced off his left shoulder; a vanilla slice gently exploded into his knees; a number of cake pops ricocheted against his chest and then a long and rather exquisitely iced Swiss roll, launched through the air like an exuberant spear, saw him completely lose his balance. As he fell, a raspberry jelly splatted gently against his nose whilst rainbow sprinkles, from the inside of one of Good Sister Honey's surprise cakes, scattered themselves across his hair and face.

And everybody watching this, from toddler to retiree, fell into a sudden and quite awe-struck silence.

Gareth gently put down Mr Weisenreider and Good Sister June.

Harold Richardson clicked the handcuffs around Dominic's wrists.

A small dollop of chocolate ganache hit William Bishop's bottom lip.

"The keys to the bakery," said Mr Weisenreider gently. "If you please, Mr Bishop."

William looked up. Almost instinctively, he licked his lips. He said, "I never knew—" And then he did not say anything else because the taste of the ganache had unlocked a perfect memory inside of him. He was standing in front of his mother and she was smiling. She had had the most beautiful smile but he had forgotten it. He had forgotten her.

And now the ganache had made him remember.

He looked up at Mr Weisenreider. He handed him the keys. "I'm sorry," he said. "I got it all wrong. All of it."

And then he looked at Good Sister June properly, for the first time since she had got out of the helicopter.

"Oh, Mr Bishop," she said. She rested her hand on his forehead. "You look like your great-aunt. I'd like to talk with you about her some time. If you're able. If you'd like."

"I don't know," said William softly. "I just don't know."

"You don't have to make a decision now," said Good Sister June as she reached into her pocket.

And ever so gently, offered him a biscuit.

A FINAL WORD FROM YOUR NARRATOR

I know that we have had a lot of endings but there is one more yet to come.[1]

And this ending begins several days later, with a conversation in the library between Good Sister June and Hanna Kowalczyk.

---

1 Good Sister Christine tells me that *The Lord of The Rings* is one of her favourite books and also has a lot of endings so Not To Worry. She also told me about how much she would quite like a pony and then said something about trying to be the first Nun of Rohan which I did not quite understand but I am still very fond of her nevertheless.

A CONVERSATION IN THE LIBRARY

Good Sister June came straight to the point. "I'm going to write about everything that's happened and put it into a book. But I want you to write the ending."

Hanna stared at her. "ME?"

"Yes."

"But why not Edie or Calla?"

"Because I want you."

"But I'm a reader. I read the books."

"I want you to do it."

Hanna took a deep breath. "I don't know where to begin," she said. "I wasn't there for half of it. All of the stuff with you when you were young? I know I found the notebook but—"

"I'll write those bits. I'll write all the stuff that you don't know or weren't there for. But I want you to take over for the final chapter."

"But why?" said Hanna.

"Because it's not my story now," said Good Sister June.

And at last, Hanna began to understand. She put down

the books that she'd been reading[1] and studied Good Sister June out of the corner of one eye. "You're not staying at the school." She had known it all along.

"No."

"I didn't think you would."

Good Sister June smiled in a rather watery fashion. "Some days, I think you are the wisest of us all."

"I had a good teacher," said Hanna. "I had you."

---

[1] *The Children of Green Knowe* by Lucy M. Boston and *The Secret Garden on 81st Street* by Ivy Noelle Weir and Amber Padilla, and if you are wondering how Hanna was reading two books at the same time, the answer is: because she is remarkably talented.

INTRODUCING

Hello.

My name is Hanna Kowalczyk.

And I'm writing the end to this book.

You should know that as much as this chapter is an end, it's also a beginning. Let me explain. Good Sister June now lives in Spun Sugar Cottage with Jessie, and together they bake cake and have people to stay. They are always people who have lost themselves a little bit and when they go back home, they've always found the bit that they've lost. I think this is because the cottage is full of very good magic and also a lot of very excellent baking. Honestly, Good Sister June is almost as good a baker as Good Sister Honey and that is High Praise Indeed.

Gareth now runs the bakery in Little Hampden. It is so perfect that it is practically Parisian, says Edie, and that is ALSO High Praise Indeed. If you are ever nearby and even if you are not, then you must call in and try his marshmallow-stuffed cookies and then his vanilla slices and then his macarons and I will STOP there before I list out the entirety of his shop because it is that perfect. He is helped in the bakery by some of the older girls who want to go into baking when they leave school and also all of the first years, who are excellent taste testers.

Oh, I forgot to mention that the bakery is only open Friday to Monday. This is because Gareth spends the other half of the week with Meredith in her cottage by the sea. The two of them are madly and fabulously in love and HOPEFULLY there will be a wedding soon because can you imagine how good the catering would be??

Also, Mr Richardson is back in charge at Little Hampden and he ended up arresting Stuart Simpson as well as the Mayor because of all the bribes that had been going around. Stuart had a guilt trip and confessed everything to him because he was given a salted caramel cupcake by one of the first years at the protest and he realized that he'd never tasted anything quite so lovely in his entire life, and really what was the point of being angry about everything any more?

The last thing you need to know about is us.

We come to Spun Sugar Cottage every weekend and when we're not learning how to bake from Good Sister June or how to thatch the cottage roof or how to light a campfire that's perfect for roasting jacket potatoes in, we're down on the beach and swimming until the water becomes spiky and sharp with cold. Then we come in and get dry and curl up like cats in the warmest spots in the house while Jessie cooks us all tea. Sometimes it's too wet and stormy for Good Sister Paulette to come and pick us up in her helicopter so we end up spending an extra night there. None of us sleep though because the entire bay comes alive with great black waves that are at least three times as high as the cottage and we spend all night watching them.

I read the last part out to Calla just now, and she has said that I sound like an author and I said well, yes, I am, I'm writing the last chapter to Good Sister June's book.

And she said, well make sure you tell them everything that they need to know,[1] like how Mr Weisenreider is now giving us all Legal Training and teaching us how to Make The Law Work For You, and how William Bishop got arrested but is atoning for his crimes in a surprisingly nice and graceful and grown-up manner. He has even been into the bakery when he's been allowed and bought a chocolate beetroot cake and he is going to stay with Good Sister June and Jessie as soon as they can work it out and I think that might actually be the best thing that has happened to him for a long time.

And I said, well, if I tell the readers all of that then I also get to tell them the cool meaningful stuff at the end like how this is a story all about feeling very sad and very lonely but also realizing that a lot of people love you and how they want you to not feel sad and lonely and all you have to do is let them in.

And I also get to tell the readers about how sometimes you might feel like everybody else is writing your story for you but really you are the one who is writing it all

[1] Like, why do ducks always need their windows fixing? The answer is: because they keep quacking the glass.

along and all you need to have is somebody to believe in you.

And after all of that, I also get to tell the readers about how I don't know what comes next in the story of Edie and Calla and me, but I do know that I'm going to make that story the best it can be and I'm going to enjoy every inch of it.

And now I'm going to go off and do precisely that.

I mean, once I've had another biscuit.

ACKNOWLEDGEMENTS

Thank you to Bryony Woods for your immeasurable support, faith, and footnote solidarity. Thank you Sarah Odedina for believing in the girls from the start and helping their stories to be the best that they can be. And a very special thank you to the lovely team at Pushkin Press. You are all beyond amazing.

Thank you to my family for everything and then everything after that as well. And also the flying saucers.

Thank you to all of the booksellers, bloggers, librarians and teachers who have supported these books and me from day one. I'm endlessly thankful for your endeavours. You're all stars.

And finally, a very special thank you to you, dear reader. Writing these books is the greatest privilege of my life. Thank you for making my dreams come true.

DAISY MAY JOHNSON

HOW TO BE

BRAVE

Why be normal when you can be happy?
PUSHKIN CHILDREN'S